the walled city

The Library of Modern Jewish Literature

Other titles in the Library of Modern Jewish Literature

the walled city

esther david

Syracuse University Press

Syracuse University Press Edition 2002
13 14 15   4 3 2

Originally published by MANAS,
an imprint of EastWest Books (Madras) Pvt. Ltd.

Published under arrangement with EastWest Books (Madras) Pvt. Ltd.,
Chennai, India.

Text illustrations by the author.

∞The paper used in this publication meets the minimum requirements
of the American National Standard for Information Sciences—Perma-
nence of Paper for Printed Library Materials, ANSI Z39.48-1992.

For a listing of books published and distributed by Syracuse University
Press, visit our website at SyracuseUniversityPress.syr.edu.

ISBN: 978-0-8156-0750-2

Library of Congress Cataloging-in-Publication Data
David, Esther.
    The walled city / Esther David—1st Syracuse University Press ed.
        p. cm. — (Library of modern Jewish literature)
    ISBN 0-8156-0750-4 (alk. paper)
    1. Mothers and daughters — Fiction. 2. Ahmadābād (India)—
    Fiction. 3. Jewish families— Fiction. 4. Women—India—Fiction.
    5. Jews—India—Fiction. I. Title. II. Series.

PR9499.3.D39 W35 2002
823—dc21   2002021081

Manufactured in the United States of America

for
Amrita and Robin

Esther David comes from a large Bene-Israel Jewish family in Ahmedabad. As a child she lived in a house by the zoo founded by her father.

She trained as a sculptor and lectures on art history at the School of Architecture, School of Interior Design, and National Institute of Fashion Technology. She was the art critic for *The Times of India*, Ahmedabad. She writes regularly for *The Indian Post*, *The Indian Express*, and Gujarati journals. She has scripted films on art for UGC programs. Formerly chairperson of the Gujarat State Lalit Kala Akademi, she is currently working for the development of art in underprivileged areas in Gujarat.

She has a son and daughter.

the walled city

me

1 940. I was born in the walled city of the fourteen gates. Walls on which the black-faced langurs with their long flag-like tails sit like sentinels, daring me to break the line of their grey bodies. Black beady eyes watch me from under long bushy Einstein brows just like Uncle Menachem's.

The river is dry, and on the banks in the empty heart of Bhadra fort, Kali waits patiently. At night, her black face and red tongue fill my dreams and sometimes her eyes flicker like the patterns in the kaleidoscope I bought at a fair.

A cow with cage-like ribs limps across the sands and rubs itself against the crumbling walls of the city. A mangy dog chases its tail in the cool shadows. They are cutting the mango trees and building a new Ahmedabad across the river. I can smell the dying fragrance of the mango blossoms. In the walled city, the houses and the pols—those narrow streets crowded with box-like tenements—grow tall and dense like trees in a rain forest, and the blazing sun burns the white mosaic on the terraces.

I go around the temple with my friend Subhadra and then, from the mandap, I look her god in the face. The white shell-eye with blood bursting at the corners scorns me. My feet stand frozen, like the dancers on the pillars; the fragrance of sandalwood paste spreads over the alcove and kindles strange desires. I peer into Subhadra's face, asking for a dot of kumkum. She looks at me questioningly and her hand remains suspended in time. The flame flickers in the brass thali and my forehead burns for the coolness of sandalwood paste.

For my mother Naomi, the bindi is an abyss. It is for her the valley of death, where she does not wish to tread. In her dreams, I drag her into the red circle with my defiant eyes. I do not know that she swims in blood. Her mother seems to call to her, and Naomi cannot answer. A kumkum circle separates them.

Back home, I fall into the pit of the sofa with my Children's Illustrated Bible. It is time for dinner when Uncle Menachem returns from the dispensary. He rules over the dining table which is laden with tall bottles of rum and plates of samosas. The smoke from his cigarette spirals across my forehead as he contemplates the lines on my hennaed palm. He looks like an ancient prophet with his huge moustache curving over his lips, his long, smooth hair parted in the middle of his forehead. He shakes his head and this scares me. My horoscope interests him and he draws lines and circles on a small piece of paper. He writes down numbers, calculates this and that and refuses to believe what he sees. I try in vain to read what the stars foretell. He sees the moonless night in my eyes and laughs, 'Lines mean nothing.' But my horoscope haunts me and I am afraid of the dark street beyond the door.

A face rises from the cigarette smoke, moving from the window into the dark night. I recognise the beggar from the Delhi Chakla bus-stand, wrapped in her dirty sari. 'Don't look at her,' says my mother every time we pass her by, but my eyes remain glued to her. What was the original colour of her sari, I wonder. Perhaps it was yellow. A single eye watches me and hands, dry and caked with dirt, stick out from a mass of rags. I can feel her hands round my neck.

I see her as a little girl with a horoscope.

Death haunts Naomi.

The leper chases her and her clothes turn into pythons that grab at her feet. She dreads the thought of being touched by the woman, as if the dirt on her hands would snatch away a comfortable home. 'Door raho,' she screams in Hindi but the homeless one moves menacingly towards her. Mother is scared and quickly throws a coin at her. The hand picks it up and rolls it on the dirty pavement, making sure that it is real.

Nervously I chew on a coin but Mother's eyes stop me. At home my knuckles are rapped for the coin could have passed through the hands of many lepers. I could get leprosy and become an outcast.

I want to return to my mother's womb.

Later Mother torments me by combing my hair. It is difficult to sit on the floor for an hour as she pats the coconut oil into my hair, removes the knots, picks out nits with her forefinger and thumb, and kills them by pressing them between her thumbnails. She arranges my hair into neat lines down my back and weaves them into an artistic braid, tying the end with a red tassel.

My neck hurts. Does the beggar woman ever comb her hair? Did her mother plait it for her? Was she ever a child? Lice from her hair migrate to mine as I doze under Naomi's oily hands.

Subhadra smiles and plays with her long, thick, black braids that are coiled like serpents in the basket of a snake charmer. Her mother also tortures her, but Subhadra says it is for her own good. How else will she become strong enough to withstand the many pregnancies to come—the fate of woman.

I cannot smile.

One winter night, a madwoman with dirt in her hair and spit rolling down her chin, lies naked on the pavement, thrashing and screaming. I dare not ask Mother why. She tries to soothe me and pretends that nobody is screaming, that the sounds mean nothing. I creep into Mani's room and snuggle into the greyness of her sari. Mani is our maid. She hears and sees things as they are. I think it is the devil screaming in the dark night.

'The woman was raped last year and now a child is being born,' Mani says. 'Men are beasts. They don't even leave a madwoman alone. The child will now belong to the street. The beggars will help.'

Under the banyan tree, next to a funerary stone, is the palm-print of an anonymous sati, perhaps another madwoman sainted after death. I return to my bed with the cry of a newborn child resounding in my ears. I wonder how Subhadra can smile so mysteriously. The dream of her unknown lover thrills her, but does she hear the screams?

Mother tries to appease me the next day, 'You did not hear anything last night. It was a bad dream and the sounds of the night are not real. We feel we hear them, but they are never there.'

I think of Naomi's world of the real and the unreal. Perhaps I was never born to her and she never knew the pain of my head tearing through her flesh. Granny says I am a gift from heaven. Mother had had two false pregnancies, and when she conceived again, they were not sure I was there, but I was. My body feels numb, as though my blood is draining out. Am I an apparition like the daughter of the chudail, the witch with the green face who sits on the tamarind tree, feet facing backwards? You cannot see her, only hear her glass bangles as she moves from one tree to another.

My stomach feels small under my dress, and I wonder how another life will form within me. There seems to be place only for me.

my working mother

Sometimes I hear the elders arguing late at night and I know of only one reason for this. Mother works as a secretary in a textile house and that seems to bother everybody. Now Granny has given an ultimatum to Father and there is tension among the elders. Father does not work and

Mother refuses to give any money towards the running of the household.

According to Granny our tiny family must also contribute its share. Father promises that he will soon find work. To avoid further discussion, he tries to persuade Mother to spend part of her salary on the house. She cries and refuses to do so, suggesting that the three of us move out instead. She feels everybody is unfair to her and says that after the closeted life she had led as a girl, it has not been easy for her to go out and work among strangers. But she works to ensure a better future for us and accuses Father of being a dreamer. I see in her eyes the fear of the street, and feel as if I am drowning in an unknown river. I cannot see myself in another house. I hope she will leave me with Granny and not force me to go with her.

Mother expects more sympathy from Granny and asks how women can survive if men abandon them. In her voice there is the memory of her own mother's fears. Granny cannot understand why a woman cannot stay at home and keep herself busy. She argues, much to Naomi's irritation, that she herself works only in the house and that that is enough.

True, my mother Naomi does less housework than Aunty Hannah or Granny. They have never become reconciled to the fact that Naomi works outside the house and earns a salary, while the rest of them have to depend on the men to take care of their expenses. The women of the house think that Mother is far too independent and they have always been a little jealous of her. Every morning, when she comes down dressed and ready to leave for work, they are already busy in the kitchen or helping our maid Fatima clean the house. During the day there are endless chores, but in the evening, when my mother comes back from work, there is nothing much for her to do, except stir the curry or set the table.

Mani and Granny look after me and everyone finds it difficult to adjust to a working woman within the family, someone who earns to support only herself. Muttering under her breath as she scrubs my back in the bathroom, Granny brands Mother mean and selfish. Aunty Hannah believes that she just sits in a chair all day long and has the best of both worlds. But Mani and Fatima sympathise with Naomi and always welcome her with a cup of tea when she returns from work.

dilhi darwaza

Black hats, fez caps, turbans, long beards and tight black suits dominate the family photograph. The elders incline their heads and look at us. The girls are in long flowing dresses with large bows in their hair and chains of beads around their necks, and the women in nine-yard saris secured between the legs. They wear nose-rings and heavy anklets, and under the frilled sleeves of their blouses their armlets gleam. I don't know where we, the younger children, will find a place in the family portrait. The family is like a huge banyan tree and we are the birds.

The house is also like a banyan tree. To reach it, one must turn to the right from Dilhi Darwaza—it is said, a Moghul emperor had returned to Delhi, royally piqued because the umbrella of his elephant had grazed the arch over the gate—, continue past the shops selling mattresses and then squeeze between the garage for the family victoria and the Syed family's three-storeyed house where there are more goats and chickens than people and where the air is always thick with the strange smell of goat droppings and jui flowers.

In this dense jungle of roofs, doors, animals, birds and sounds, the houses appear small and they always open into a courtyard with a tree or a few plants. Houses with roofs high and low, form a network that links various parts of the walled city. Cool, congested, yet inviting, the buildings rise tall and spread from lane to lane and the odours of curry swim from one house to another.

The large wooden doors of our house painted green, with red lotus knockers, are often kept closed, so that stray dogs do not come in. To enter the house one pushes open the wicket gate which is locked only in the afternoons when Uncle Menachem takes a nap. There is a lavatory by the doorstep, and the thin, stooped sweeper Kalu, who wears khaki shorts, collects the drums every morning at ten, empties them into his wheelbarrow, and takes away the nightsoil who knows where.

'The curse of his caste, says Mani.

Granny's cousin Gerard lives across the street and his son Joel, the long-haired body-builder, stands on the terrace in the morning sun, massaging his bulging biceps with mustard oil. He is our uncle and is preparing to compete for the title of Mr.Gujarat. He has the right build for that. Cousin Malkha watches him from the corner of her eye while pretending to do her homework. He resembles a Greek god as he bends over from the waist to lift weights. Malkha cannot resist him and writes him a love letter. I know something happened to Malkha after she went for the morning show of 'Samson and Delilah' at Central Cinema.

From her bed Granny watches every move that Malkha makes. In fact, everybody seems to be watching Malkha. Granny recently discovered a red stain on the grey-tiled bathroom floor. A little red spot which has darkened Malkha's existence. She looks sad, and complains of stomachaches; Amina our fat cook prepares hot water bottles and giggles about Malkhababy's marriage. Malkha glares at her and tries to watch Joel from the window. They exchange looks of longing, and in her dreams, Malkha walks into Joel's arms.

In the verandah of Great Uncle Gerard's house is a huge wooden coop where Anwar and Father keep their pigeons. It is bigger than Anwar's house next door. Anwar is Father's friend and works all day long with his brothers, sitting hunched on the ground, chiselling perfect square stone tiles in the open yard in front of his house. Together, Father and he look after the birds, discussing them all the time, even while Anwar works. They have a fine collection of Pouter pigeons which they let out in the evenings to show off their proud strutting walk. Father is not allowed to keep birds in the house. Granny says it is too much work and he laughs and accepts her decision. It is good to enter the house to the cooing of pigeons.

I think the kitchen is the soul of the house, because that's where the water pots are kept. When we come into it from the sun, it is like diving into the belly of a green coconut. The brass ladle clangs against the pot as we pour out water into the silver glasses.

Granny, Aunty Hannah and Amina spend endless hours around the huge oven which is plastered with yellow clay from the river and fed with coal and logs of wood. Only they know the secret of keeping the fire burning at the right temperature.

Near the windows and suspended from the ceiling, onions and garlic trapped in big net bags sprinkle their dry skin on us. Peeling is an activity that needs many hands. The women sit at the dining table for hours and shred, grate and cry over mounds of onions. Fatima, hunched over the pestle, grinds the garlic and ginger paste so perfectly that the curry melts in the mouth. Aunty Hannah watches over her shoulder and tests the masala till it reaches the smoothness she wants.

The dishes are stacked on shelves ranged against the wall. The huge meat safe protects the milk, yogurt and leftover food from flies and cats. Mother thinks the kitchen is cluttered and messy. She prefers to use a kerosene stove or cooking gas, and stainless steel dishes.

The nicer china bowls, porcelain vases and glassware from the time of Queen Victoria's coronation, are displayed in rosewood cupboards with glass panes. They are so precious that they may be touched only by the hands of the women of the house.

There is a huge teakwood dining table with heavy legs and generations of old stains. There is a fixed place for everyone. Uncle sits at the head of the table and Father sits on the opposite side. Aunty Hannah irritates Mother by taking the place of authority opposite Granny and nearer the stove. To me the dining table seems like a room in itself.

Uncle Menachem cannot imagine lunch or dinner without gulab jamuns or pedas. He winks and says it is not permissible to mix milk and meat, but he cannot help it. We do not know what he is talking about. His son Samuel explains to us the rules of traditional cooking, shamelessly eating a milk peda with a meat samosa. He says, 'In our house we do not marinate meat in curd. We do not cook the lamb in its mother's milk. In a way we obey the law, or at least try to.'

Every alternate day it is Fatima's duty to buy samosas from Khamasa Gate, on the steps of Rani Sipri's mosque. They are supposed to be the best in the city but the brothers continue to argue over whether the Pankor Naka samosas are better than the Sipri ones.

fairies and pimps

I n the house at Dilhi Darwaza the windows are closed only at night or on hot summer afternoons. Through their iron bars, in a perpetual flurry of light and sound, the street enters the house and becomes a part of our lives. Bhuriben, the Rabari woman, calls out to Mani in the early hours of the morning, balancing on her head the shining brass pots of fresh milk. Mani tells the time by the calls of the different vendors on their rounds and her world is disturbed when a regular does not pass by.

Jingling bangles, colourful tassels and embroidered hand fans; the smell of new brooms, raw mangos, fresh vegetables, green mint, pink candy floss; the forbidden cart with the coloured bottles of sherbet, pots full of kulfi, pickles and freshly grated ice gola dripping with rose syrup lend a richness to our lives.

There is nothing Mani likes better than haggling with the broom seller who calls out in a funny nasal whine. The bhaiya who sells us vegetables knows her well and refuses to sell her anything if she tells him to bring down his price. He argues that vegetables are expensive and that he has to send money to his wife in Mathura.

Late every afternoon, Mani waits in the backyard for Kamla the Vaghri trader, who barters old clothes for new aluminium vessels. Kamla cannot afford to travel by bus since she has six hungry children and instead, walks through the streets of Ahmedabad with her burden of clothes and vessels. When she reaches our house, she sits under the shade of the neem tree and Mani joins her there with a glass of water and a bidi and keeps her company until she finishes her lunch of dry bajri rotla and a green chilli which she brings wrapped in a cloth. Between them exists the sympathy of travellers.

Aunty Hannah grudges Mani her afternoons under the neem tree. The family washing is dried in the backyard and she suspects that Kamla is a thief and thinks that Mani steals clothes from the house, passes them on to her and gets a share of the spoils. I feel a constriction in my throat when Aunty Hannah accuses Mani of stealing a dress that has probably been misplaced. Mani keeps silent, and her expression remains hurt and withdrawn until the dress is found.

Mani uses the side door of the dining room which opens into the backyard. She tells me that she feels imprisoned when the back door is locked at night. Aunty Hannah is paranoid about Kamla entering the house.

The courtyard is also a sort of parlour and the men sit around here on string cots. The hookah changes hands and guests are entertained with tea and sweet biscuits, or the rice cakes that Mother sometimes bakes. I prefer the Gujarati chevado which Mother is now learning to make from Subhadra's mother.

Upstairs, there is another drawing room that Uncle Menachem uses as a temporary clinic and library. It is also my parents' winter bedroom. The hexagonal table with the carved lion paws is moved aside, their mattresses are brought in, and they sleep with the smell of tincture-iodine wafting around them. Father's rifle and dilruba stand in a corner. Sometimes they wake to the sounds of patients banging on the door, howling with pain.

A narrow staircase of Burma teak leads to the open terrace where you can dream uninterrupted. There are rooms on the left and a mosaic-domed birdbath as well. It is a place that nobody cares to use or clean and against the sunset it gives the house the silhouette of a palace. I scrape my heels on the dry droppings of pigeons and glance at the room near the landing as I turn to leave.

It is a storeroom, cluttered with neatly folded mattresses and quilts, phlegm-stained pillows, bags of old cotton, expensive carpets, silver rose water sprinklers, black iron trunks full of old clothes, torn paper kites, a charkha, an old harmonium, moth balls, mousetraps, dry neem leaves, huge copper cauldrons and sepia-tinted framed photographs of unknown relations like the faded clots of blood on a mouldy quilt. Granny keeps the key to this room in a key-bunch that hangs from her waist on a silver hook.

Uncle Menachem, large-hearted that he is, lends the backyard to Subhadra's family and the Patels, for weddings and rituals like the naming of newborn babies. And on some nights, Mehboob Khan or the Syed family or Anwar's cousins hold a feast in our backyard to celebrate a wedding or a circumcision.

Biryani cooks in large blackened pots on open fires and the night grows heady with the flavour of saffron. Eunuchs dance and people throw coins at them. They wear pink and blue brocade saris and strings of jasmine are woven into their long false braids. They make obscene gestures, pick up their saris and show their thick hairy legs. We watch in amazement. Then a girl takes over and sings provocative lyrics in a high-pitched nasal voice. Sometimes, in the middle of a stanza, she stands up with her hands held over her head and shakes her hips. The crowd swoons. She stoops to collect the currency notes they throw at her and bends in an elaborate salaam, then gives herself a breather. She chews paan, spits the red juice and continues to sing till the early hours of the morning. We admire the courage with which she sings all alone among so many men.

To me the singing girls and the eunuchs look alike. But I'm sure they must be different. The girls do not clap their hands like the eunuchs, with their fingers spread out and palms clashing together like cymbals. Instead, they make delicate gestures with their hands and show their alta-coloured ankles adorned with the circle of silver bells.

In loud whispers Cousin Samuel tells us all about the eunuchs. Hiding in the darkness and huddled at the window which opens into the backyard, we listen to him. They kidnap young boys, he says, and then in front of the goddess Bahucharaji who rides a rooster, they castrate them with a knife. If they survive, they become like women and begin to dress like them. Samuel's eyes are round with fear.

I would hate to see Samuel suffer like that. Anyway he is very careful when he goes out into the street. He steers clear of anyone suspicious who could kidnap him and transform him into a eunuch or a maimed beggar. But if it happened how would we ever recognize Samuel again ? Of course he knows our address, but what if we changed house? Besides we would be grown up and no longer look like little frogs! Samuel warns us that little girls are also kidnapped and turned into singing girls and we cling to each other.

Our eyes are dazzled by a sudden light. Aunty Hannah stands with her hand on the switch. Outside, a girl in a red sari with a design of green mangos continues to dance. We turn back for one last look, and I notice that she has a black velvet purse swinging from her arm. Caught in our midnight escapade, we return to bed. Aunty is upset with Uncle Menachem for allowing the neighbours to use our backyard. We the corrupted, fall into a fitful sleep and dream of fairies and pimps.

kites and scorpions

In the morning, we drag ourselves to school. At lunchtime the kites swoop down on my pickle-soaked chapati. As I take a bite and keep my eyes on their flight, the thought of their sharp claws gouging out my eyes and the blood splashing on my red-checked uniform makes me throw the chapatis at them. They are leftovers from the night before and the heat of the afternoon has made them rancid. There is never any time in the morning to make something fresh. The swooping bird makes a somersault and catches a piece in mid-air.

Mother opens my lunch box and a stale, acrid smell hits me. Did I eat enough, she asks. My stomach rumbles and Shirin's lunch floats in front of my eyes. It comes in a car, neatly packed in a tiffin carrier. The chauffeur lays out the steaming rice, dal and vegetables on a white cloth, complete with the silver. As Shirin eats and blinks at us absently, the chauffeur drives away the kites.

I cannot pay attention to Sister Josephina's geography lesson. I wonder how it feels to be always hungry, and to live on the cold pavement. At least I can look forward to a hot, steaming dinner. Amina makes delicious mutton curry and roasts hot chapatis on the iron griddle.

I find it a bother to study on an empty stomach and make a mistake in my arithmetic homework. I munch the stale dry chapati I find in the meat safe. Mani scolds me and wants to give me a fresh one. 'That,' she says, 'is for the sweeper woman, when she comes to ask for leftover food.' At dinnertime, the food sticks in my throat. Uncle says I have worms.

Later, in the coalroom, a scorpion stings Amina's hand and she screams. Uncle applies a drop of some sort of acid and cauterises the sting with a lighted matchstick. Tears stream down her fat cheeks as her hand swells and she asks Allah to forgive her. She wonders if she is going to die. Naomi tells her, 'Nobody dies of a scorpion's sting.' I blow on her hand and she smiles. Mani murmurs, 'You suffer in this birth for the sins of your last birth. The pavements are full of people suffering for the sins of their past life.' I thrash about in my sleep. The sins of my past life keep me hungry in this life. Most nights I go to bed without a proper dinner. I eat too much chana and drink too much water or an interesting conversation distracts me.

The only time I seem to eat well is at Subhadra's house. Sometimes after school we play together. At seven in the evening, when preparations for dinner have not yet started at home, the food is ready to be served in Subhadra's house. I refuse her invitation, saying that I have eaten a snack and that I will eat dinner later. But she hears the rumbling in my stomach and forces me to eat. Her mother will not allow a meat-eater like me inside the kitchen where a lamp burns in front of the family deity. So we sit in the mosaic-tiled drawing room and eat from brass thalis. I smell for hours on my fingers the hot Gujarati dal, basmati rice, sour potato curry and the sweet and sour mango pickle. I hope Mother doesn't find out that I've eaten there. As a rule, the family eats together after the men return and have had their rum and soda.

The hair inside Mani's nose twitches with anxiety. She feels that I should not be too friendly with Subhadra. We are different, she adds as an afterthought. I can never understand her when she talks like that. I try hard to keep away from Subhadra, but she is my best friend. We grew up together. But the meat of dead animals sticks to my teeth and the camphor on her breath rejects me. Between us there is a wall of dead animals and birds.

On hot summer afternoons she comes to my house and then runs back to her own to drink water. Her nose twitches at our kitchen smells. I am ridden with guilt for the ways of my ancestors. I wish I had been born to Subhadra's mother, I would have then been accepted.

We go to the synagogue on Friday evenings with Granny. I am nervous and long to play with the Star of David around her neck. It is very difficult to tell her that the Hebrew prayers bore me. I do not understand the meaning of the words. For hours I stand next to her and fidget with the ends of her sari.

Subhadra sings her prayers in the little pooja alcove and she knows what they mean. She rings a little brass bell, moving it in circles around the pictures of her gods and lights agarbattis. As we flip through the pages of the old Hebrew prayer book, she asks me the meaning of my prayers. I do not know what they mean.

Her finger traces a name written in Marathi in heavy ink with a quill pen. It says Dandekar. She asks me the meaning of the name. I hesitate; it is my family name. Quickly I tell her that we do not use it. It hangs somewhere in the inner world of my memory, with the tales of ancestors shipwrecked on the Konkan coast, reciting the Hebrew prayers silently and becoming one with the people there, wearing Indian clothes, speaking the local language and taking a new name, the name of the surrogate village that had adopted them.

I look at my image in the mirror. I am but a wisp of that memory and sometimes I question my Jewishness. My complexion is a deep brown like Subhadra's and my long plait is tied with red tassels. I could be her sister.

Naomi and Aunty Hannah have lighter skin. Granny, in fact, has pink cheeks. But then there are many with dark skin like mine at the synagogue. Mother says it is because I play in the sun and rubs a paste of fresh cream and chana ata on my face to lighten my skin. Samuel and I search for features similar to ours in the Children's Illustrated Bible.

Granny wears the nine-yard sari in the Maharashtrian style, and covers her head. She speaks to us in Marathi. We answer her in Gujarati. She always scolds Hannah and Naomi for not teaching us enough Marathi. It is our mother tongue, she says. We ask her to write her name and she giggles like a little girl. The written word eludes her. Like most Indian women of her generation she was not sent to school. Aunty Hannah is ashamed that her mother-in-law's signature is a thumb impression and boasts of her own proficiency in English and French. Yet Granny astonishes us by fluently reciting the Hebrew prayers. She insists we repeat them after her, and our lips move with hers.

Hannah and Naomi wear the sari in the modern Indian style, with the pallav on the left shoulder. They wear gold and glass bangles on the right arm and delicate Rolex watches on their left wrist. Their long black hair, heavily oiled, tied into long plaits and woven into an elaborate bun, sits at their nape. On festivals and weddings a string of small chrysanthemums decorates the bun, a sign of their Konkani tradition.

Subhadra wonders why my mother does not wear the red kumkum dot on her forehead. Her mother looks beautiful in a sari worn Gujarati style across the right shoulder and tucked at the waist. There is always a bright red bindi between her brows.

The sun blazes like a huge dot in the sky. Subhadra makes a perfect dot on my virginal forehead, and some of the kumkum dust falls in a thin line on the bridge of my nose.

Naomi's eyes bore into the middle of my forehead. The wooden scale raps my knuckles and the blood rushes from my hand to my head. Later, when Mani is alone, I look at her bare forehead and tell her that she'd look beautiful with a dot. She is shocked and convinced that Subhadra is an evil influence on me. 'Our religions,' she says, 'do not permit such rituals.' I dare not ask why.

In my dreams, I draw the bindi in a thousand and one ways, with powder, paste and glue. The circle must be complete if you wish to open the third eye.

'That's crazy,' says Subhadra. 'When Shiva opens his third eye, the world is destroyed.'

I wonder whether the great flood and Noah had anything to do with the third eye. I see tongues of fire in Shiva's long tresses, and dread to think of the floods that he could unleash. To me, his foot, suspended in space and balanced in perfect symmetry, is beautiful.

When I lift my foot so as not to tread on the dirty sari of the beggar woman, I wonder if I have the power to destroy her. But she sits there, already destroyed, caught in the web of fate. Does she also pray to her gods with a little tinkling bell before she leaves to beg? 'Late in the night,' says Mani,' she cooks some khichdi for herself, and sometimes people throw leftover food into her bowl.' The tea vendor across the road always gives her tea in the morning and calls her 'Ma'. When he has leftover bhajias he gives them to her, sometimes with raw papaya chutney, and tells her to eat them before the dogs smell the food and snatch it from her hand. But she has learnt to keep them away by throwing a few morsels at them. Late at night, one of the more friendly dogs sleeps in the curve of her body.

I ask Mani how she knows all about the beggar, and she explains that her favourite bidi shop is near the Dariapur bus-stand where the woman begs for alms. If it were not for Granny, Mani would have also been on the streets. Perhaps she likes to gaze upon the fate she has escaped. 'Before your birth,' she says to me, 'I became homeless, during the communal riots.' She refers to them by the simple word komi, which always sounds like an era.

She has made a place for herself in the storeroom between the drums of wheat, rice and dal and sleeps on the thin patchwork quilt she herself has made with colourful rags and old saris. I am afraid for her and wonder how she prevents the centipedes that crawl into the room from entering her ears. Mani says, once inside your head they could have families in there and you would not even know about it, but would slowly become mad. I do not feel safe in my bed and dread to think that they could fall into my ear from the ceiling. I climb into Granny's bed. Instinctively she opens her breasts to me.

silver anklets

other often seems uncomfortable with us. When I say us, I mean my father's family. She grew up in a different environment and does not belong here, in this house. She has lived in the same city, but her early life had been different from ours. In her father's house the sweeper does not make rounds to collect drums of nightsoil, nor do the maids sit around and gossip. The street is not a thoroughfare to their house.

'Being like the British' obsesses my grandfather Daniel. He used to work for a British-owned company and affected the mannerisms of his bosses. Yet in a strange way, Indian life and customs too fascinate him.

I am sucked into the labyrinths of his life, although I am taken to see him only once a week on Sunday afternoons. We sit on the swing and I watch his bald head and think of Subhadra's lustrous hair, while he helps me put on a pair of silver anklets. We laugh when I move my feet and the silver bells jingle.

Mohun, the man who looks after Danieldada, applies a red dot on Dada's shining forehead. Grandmother Leah had been terrified of the kumkum bindi. It had been the colour of her nightmares. As Mohun bends towards me, Mother's slap echoes in my ears and I move away to study the peacock in the brass chain of the swing, for in his hand is a brass plate with a clay lamp, kumkum powder in a silver box, and pedas. I know this is his daily routine of aarti. Danieldada has given him a room, the walls of which he has covered with pictures of gods. His favourite is the cute little Ganesh. I like the smiling elephant too. Will my mother materialise on the verandah now, look angrily at the thali and at me, and turn upon her own father with hatred in her eyes? She feels that Mohun is given too much liberty, and cannot understand why Grandfather allows him to have a pooja room for his gods in what is, after all, a Jewish house.

The spell of pleasure is broken. Naomi is upset with Danieldada for having bought me the anklets. According to her, Jewish girls should wear no ornaments, except perhaps a chain, a brooch, a watch or bangles. Besides, young girls like me should not be given such expensive gifts. Dada is hurt. He unhooks the anklets, wraps them in a piece of red paper, and carefully replaces them in a little red box. He will keep them for me to wear when I visit him. He likes the sound of silver bells. I want to scream, 'Give me back my anklets!' I twist the chain of the swing, strangling the peacock and the parrot. Danieldada smiles sadly as I pull on my socks and shoes. I walk stiffly with Naomi to the victoria and all the way back she explains to me the correct dress and behaviour codes for Jewish girls. Phrases with a series of 'don'ts' fly around my ears, but I am thinking of other things. Anyway, I could not have worn anklets with shoes. Perhaps I could have.

I am confused. I decide to ask Granny about anklets and Jewishness. I remember finding an old sepia-tinted photograph of Granny as a thoughtful young girl standing with her arms folded near a vase of artificial flowers placed on a stand. She is wearing a nose-ring. Ballerina-like, she balances on one foot while the other, adorned by a heavy, chain-like anklet is visible below the hem of her skirt. Anklets and nose-ring don't seem to have affected her.

I need to hold my mother, but her starched sari repels me. In my mind I hold on to Ganesh with his nice round stomach. It is comforting to look into his affectionate eyes, although perhaps he too is a little short-sighted like all elephants. Samuel tells

me that all the animals of the world will disappear very soon.
He laughs at me when I tell him that we will always have Ganesh,
then asks me why I use the word 'we'. I tell him that I use it in
the same way Mani does. Samuel says seriously that all religious
texts are different but he does not know how and I surprise him
by telling him of the similarities between the stories of Krishna
and Moses.

We ask Uncle Menachem, and he broods over the question.
He says that Mani has a Bible similar to ours, though not
entirely. We have the same father in Abraham and we have
the same prophets. Only the way we say the names is different.
He sees that we are not entirely convinced and questions us
about the difference between a temple and a synagogue. We
tell him that the synagogue has no idols, while a temple has
human figures with weapons and flowers. I dread to tell him
that I find the colourful and noisy Hindu temple an easier
place to pray in. The synagogue is silent and I can never
decide on one point, one central bindu, on which to focus my
attention. Although afraid of his reaction, I ask him why we
cannot have the picture of a bearded prophet in the synagogue,
and suddenly my thoughts turn to the compassionate eyes of
Christ in the chapel of my convent school. I had always felt
sorry for him until my classmate Elizabeth had looked
strangely at me and accused me of being the 'you people'.

Uncle Menachem is not listening to me, his attention is
focused on Granny lighting the Shabbat candles. A white silk
tablecloth embroidered with the word shalom is kept aside for
Shabbat and the kaddish prayers. We always look forward to

the days when we cover our heads with handkerchiefs and stand, pushing against the table, while Uncle Menachem says the prayers and lifts the crocheted cloth to bless the flaked rice, washed well and mixed with rose petals, raisins and sugar. There are dates to remind us of the desert, bananas and apples, unsalted omelettes and sweet puris made of wheat flour and jaggery, deep fried in pure ghee. The jar is full of wine made from black currants soaked the night before, then boiled, cooled and crushed with Granny's own hands. The bread, freshly baked in the clay oven, is on the table and the salt is in a small blue plate. With each Hebrew sentence we pick up the dates and the apples, just the way Uncle does, one after the other. The words mean nothing to us. We are allowed to ask Uncle Menachem all the questions we want to before the Shabbat candles are lit. After that he sits brooding and re-reads stray parts from the Bible to himself. Then, as Aunty Hannah and Mother bring in the steaming soup plates filled to the brim, he blesses in Hebrew the bread and the salt and we wait to be served.

No sooner do the prayers end than the whole family scatters to different parts of the house. But they make it a point to come to the table and kiss the glow of the candle with their fingers. Amina, Mani and Fatima also kiss the flame. Uncle Menachem and Father remember to wear the tiny, gold-embroidered, blue skull caps. Father keeps silent during the prayers. He says he has forgotten the words. Sometimes, he even forgets to kiss the candle flame and has to be reminded to do so.

Soon we may have to live in Danieldada's house. He is nice to be with, but I dread the thought of living there with my mother. The tension between her and my grandfather troubles me.

The silences of inner anger burst into screams and accusations. The sun is never as hot as it is on such days. The river is turbulent, and the fish die. We lie quietly in bed, staring at the ceiling. A lizard crawls there upside down and I wonder whether it is me on the ceiling and the lizard on the bed. We stare at each other, seeming to move in strange circles. A lizard falling on the head, says Mani, brings death.

I am afraid of becoming motherless. But then my mother does not have a mother either. She died young.

I would feel like an orphan without Mani.

shahibagh

 The chameleon turns from red to yellow in Danieldada's garden.

I am not sure if I like the silence of Shahibagh. Once in a while we can hear the peacocks in Shah Jahan's palace. A heron stands silently on one leg in the thin line of water in the middle of the river bed.

I miss the bustle and activity of the big house and the crowded street of Delhi Chakla. Here no one dares to enter the house. Mohun keeps a strict watch on the door from the kitchen window.

The school bus picks me up at the gate of the house and I don't think I will ever make friends here. I feel awkward in my rather ill-fitting clothes. The girls of Shahibagh dress well but Mother insists on my wearing these matronly clothes. It seems as though she thinks my body is sinful and has to be hidden. The belt around the ribcage suffocates me.

I realize that Uncle Menachem is not my father and Granny is not my mother. Suddenly I am face to face with my own father. We are both like aliens in my mother's house. On hot afternoons we yearn for the other house. Strapping iron grips on his trousers, my father escapes on his bicycle to the old house under the pretext of looking after his pigeons. I would like to ask him to take me with him but he keeps his eyes averted. He does not want me to get too attached to the old house.

From the swing in the verandah I follow Father with my eyes in much the same way that I gaze at the street leading to Granny's house when the school bus passes that way. If only I could be sick near the old house, then the bus would have to stop and I could request the conductor to drop me off there.

This never happens even though my head throbs whenever we near the Dilhi Darwaza crossroads. I always see the beggar woman and sometimes Mani at the meat shop smoking a bidi. I almost call out to her, but I worry about the smart Shahibagh girls. The water spills from my water bottle as we drive past the masjid of Rani Roopmati. At the ghodagadi stand, the sharp smell of horse urine hits us. The girls' handkerchiefs are already out but I can never find mine.

I look forward to the days when there is nobody at home in Shahibagh. Then I am dropped off at Granny's and when she is chatting with Ruksanabibi in the courtyard, I crawl into Mani's quilt of colours. 'The mosque walks,' she says, 'and so it is called Chalte Pir ki Dargah. Every year they take measurements and it has always moved a centimetre. If you wish for something, you tie a string at the lattice window. The wish comes true if you believe in the holy spirit who lives there. The spirit moves below the green cloth strewn with red roses.'

I wonder if my other grandmother Leah had also asked the spirit a favour. In a green sari with red roses, worn over a frilly white silk blouse, she walks out of her bromide portrait in Danieldada's room and I see her, round-faced and plump, tying a string at the lattice window. She moves from one trellis window to another, always asking the spirits to free her husband from the arms of another woman.

I find it difficult to believe, looking at this nice old man who is my grandfather, that he could ever torture anyone. He seems so gentle when he ties my laces or struggles with the hooks of my uniform. Yet I see a certain resentment in his eyes when he looks at my mother, his daughter. Memories of my grandmother Leah's unrealized wishes haunt them. I have never seen her. In the bromide photograph, she looks as beautiful and loving as Granny. They say my hair curls as naturally as hers did.

pollen

I n March the air is thick with pollen from the mango flowers. It is Holi. Mother would like to lock me up in a cupboard. She does not open the door to my neighbour Pratibha who calls out to me, dripping wet with colours.

The colours fascinate Danieldada. He says that he is too

old to play Holi but would like me to. He takes some sindoor from Mohun's pooja room and dabs my cheeks with it. We look on with horror as a sprinkling of orange specks stains my powder blue dress. We try to wash it off but a deep pink stain remains.

We are running in the tunnel below Kali's feet and Naomi seems to chase us in the dark with a sword. We do not see her. She is there and not there, but we sense her presence around us. I feel the cold sweat on Dada's palm.

At the dining table Naomi notices the pink patch. Her face hardens and over my head her eyes meet Danieldada's. He smiles mischievously and tells my father that if it weren't for his age he would still play Holi with such abandon that he would shame the youngsters running down the street.

Danieldada pours for himself and Father yet another glass of bhang that Mohun has concocted for him with hemp flowers, rose leaves, variali, milk and a coin thrown in for whatever effect.

Much to Mother's disapproval, Father drinks with Danieldada, glass for glass. Their eyes sparkle, the kesuda flower blossoms on their cheeks and their laughter gurgles like the Sabarmati river in spate. I laugh with them. Kesuda, the tree of spring is in bloom—the leaves have fallen and the blood-red flowers with velvet tongues stand upright on the thorny tree. When the bhang goes to his head, Danieldada orders Mohun to soak the kesuda flowers in water. It makes the most beautiful orange colour. Naomi is angry and eats her lunch as though she is in a hurry but the puri rolls around in my throat and refuses to go down. She leaves the table with tears in her eyes, imploring Grandfather not to corrupt 'her' family and laments that we don't celebrate Purim anymore.

I see myself in my mind's eye dressed for Purim as Queen Esther in a flowing maroon robe with a smock of silver embroidery and a paper crown sitting on my unbound hair. Just like the picture in our little Bible. I hope Cousin Malkha does not dress up as the Queen as well. I want Mother to buy me a better dress than Malkha's for the fancy dress party at the synagogue. Granny says that we should dress in Indian costumes, and that I would look perfect either as a Konkani fisherwoman from the scene of our shipwreck, or a 'cultured' Bengali lady. I refuse to listen to her.

I want to be a queen. I miss Samuel and our joint daydreaming games. I am sure he will dress as Mordecai. He likes to boast that he understands everything.

The oil in my tightly plaited hair has a strange stale smell that moves in a circle around my head, like a halo. Mother never allows me to leave my hair loose, even for a fancy dress party at the synagogue.

Anyway we can go to the synagogue only if Granny sends the victoria. That is, if she invites us to join them. I am not sure whether Granny wants to see my mother but I am certain she will send Mani to fetch me.

We always end up sitting as spectators in our ordinary clothes. The boys in khaki knickerbockers and white shirts, the girls in pink or blue frilly dresses hanging over their knees. Our polished shoes shine like the oil in our hair. In our dreams we are the superior queens and kings looking down at commoners.

Danieldada tells me how he used to try to persuade his three daughters and wife Leah to play Holi. But Leah was convinced

that there was something terribly un-Jewish about celebrating
the festival of another religion because it meant being unfaithful
to hers.

The happy screams of girls drenched in water, running wildly
with colour in their hair, somehow seemed sinful to her.

If only my mother could open herself to the blaze of colours
and the fragrance of pollen in her hair.

It is difficult to believe that Danieldada could have lived
without the discipline of Jewish family life. In the photograph
of his younger days, he looks every inch the pucca British officer
in a well-tailored suit, sitting regally on an elaborately carved
wooden chair. A short coat, tight at the waist, a tie held with a
diamond pin, a rose in his lapel. His tiny dagger-shaped
moustache turns up at the corners and his hair is well lacquered
and combed in waves. He says he used to wear patent leather
shoes specially made by a Chinese shoemaker on Relief Road.

Samuel is impressed and says that he has class.

Danieldada insists on eating with a knife and fork. We
continue to eat with our fingers and I try to use a napkin as he
does. I would like to learn to eat like him but Mother seems not
to care. She senses my attraction for Grandfather's ways and
tells me that he'd been no different, even when her mother was
alive. When Naomi speaks like that, I know that she will not
allow any discussion on the subject.

Words come easily to Grandfather, specially at dinnertime.
He dresses for dinner, rubs his favourite Yardley's eau de cologne
on his jaws, and sits majestically at the head of the table, a peg
of whisky in front of him. He chats with Mohun who always

stands to his right, much to Mother's disgust. Father and I listen attentively but Mother remains aloof.

At times, Mother shoots a poison arrow at Danieldada and asks him why he had never talked to her mother as he does to Mohun.

He does not answer, nor does he stop talking. When he tells a story he never looks at Mother. Sometimes his eyes linger on the water stains on my legs. I never seem to wash well enough when I return from school. Strange how tear stains also look the same.

Mother tells Danieldada that on Holi she spent hours washing the stains off the bathroom floor and his clothes.

Colours fade in their eyes.

Coils of tensions weave between us in our little cottage in Shahibagh. In the old house I had never sensed them, though they must have existed even there. Here they seem to have come closer, roping me in. I feel myself falling.

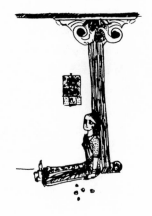

cowrie shells
on mosaic floors

I am waiting for the school bus. High up above me, a girl as old as I am, walks gingerly on a tightrope. Her straggly unkempt hair falls over her eyes, and the torn over-sized dress hangs all over her. The girl's father plays the drum and her mother collects coins in the cup of her hands. Grime has cut a black gash across her fate line.

I wait for the summer vacation. Granny misses me. I long to curl up in my favourite corner in the old house. Mother says that I am like a cat, caring more for houses than for people. I worry and feel guilty about liking the house. Of course I like people just as much.

Subhadra's eyes hold a vision of Kali. She imagines her holding a sword, wearing a waistband of skulls. Suddenly our lives have changed. I don't know why. Subhadra has changed. She now wears a long skirt and a half-sari. I am shocked to see her hair cropped short because of the lice which infest it. She can no longer play with her long plaits. There was always something sacred about her hair. Whenever we played with cowrie shells, I was careful not to touch my head to hers. Now, without her plaits, she looks like her brother.

I realize that somewhere along the way we must have grown up. Subhadra has stopped going to school and her mother hints at an engagement. I look at my school dress and feel that I haven't grown and Subhadra is already a woman. Anyway, she has always been ahead of me. While I could not even light the stove, Subhadra could make beautiful round chapatis, fry puris and cut bhindi perfectly. In our own house, we children are told to keep away from fire, knives and electric gadgets.

Subhadra's mother feels that if I spend some time with her, she might feel better. I spread out the cowrie shells on the mosaic floor for a game that I know Subhadra likes. As I throw the dice, she stares at the white shells on the floor, then gathers them up and throws them away. I pick up the dice and put them into the wooden box. I think our childhood is over. Unlike before, the cowrie shells now look like lips, hiding the mysteries of our lives.

I look into Subhadra's expressionless eyes lined with homemade kohl. She looks distant like Goddess Durga in the picture which hangs in her house. I feel like bowing down to touch her feet, the way I have seen her touch the feet of her gods. I want to run away.

The centipedes must have entered Subhadra's ears. They must have been attracted by the scented oil her mother rubs into her scalp to make her hair grow again. Subhadra's hair is plastered so heavily with marrow oil mixed with gooseberries that it appears to be shining with a purplish lacquer. The oil runs down from her forehead to her ears in a green line and I am sure this is what attracted the centipedes.

I blame her mother for the misfortune.

According to Mani, a head full of lice is the haunt of ghosts. I dare not bring back lice. If I did, Mother would rip the hair from my scalp with a short-toothed wooden comb.

Subhadra's mother showers me with sweet smiles and offers me a plate of crisp methi khakhras with a piece of sweet-sour raw mango pickle marinated in mustard oil. She knows she is the best cook in the world. When she leaves for the temple, Subhadra lifts her skirt over her calf. I expect to see a new pair of silver anklets, but instead I see her leg branded with the iron tongs her mother uses to move the coal in the clay stove. My eyes fill with tears and the mango does not taste good any more. She wants to go back to school but her family wants her to marry a boy she has never seen. Subhadra is afraid.

She is not thrilled about her unknown lover.

Mani tells me about the screams and shouts she hears from Subhadra's house. Late one night, when she had been sitting on the footpath smoking a bidi, Mani had heard Subhadra pleading with her parents to let her become a doctor. She is good at maths and science. Her mother tells her that she herself was married at five and had never gone to school. Subhadra will be thirteen and at least knows how to read and write.

Mani sighs, and tells me how she was engaged when she was in her mother's womb. She feels that evil spirits might have entered Subhadra's body when she was walking under the tamarind tree at the twilight hour. Weak with too much weeping, Subhadra must have been an easy prey. Everyone thinks she'll feel better once she is married.

The Sidis walk past our house, with camphor burning in an earthen jar, held by a huge black woman. Her head is covered, and she wears a long dress. The men in lungis wave huge peacock feather brooms and the other men and women in the group chant something. They move as if in a trance. Uncle Menachem says that they are from Abyssinia, that their ancestors had come to India as slaves for the Nawab of Junagadh. 'And once upon a time,' he says, 'they ruled over Ahmedabad.'

I look up the map and see that by Abyssinia Uncle means Ethiopia. A little part of mysterious Africa circles our house every day.

Subhadra shivers when she hears them pass by. Her mother stops them and gives them alms and they bless the house.

Subhadra has been taken to the exorcist at the slum on the river bed in Shahpur. Her ears resound with the beat of the goat-intestine drums. Her eyes are red from the smoke of the chilli powder thrown into the fire. Her mother says, the evil spirit inside Subhadra screamed, 'I am going,' and then left her.

I sit on the floor, waiting for her to get up so that we can play some game or the other, but she seems to be sleeping.

In the busy Dariapur area, there is a temple with a garden of young chikoo trees and a small lily pond.

'It was there,' says Mani, 'that they found Subhadra's body floating among the white lilies.' 'But the pond is too small for suicide,' she adds with a hint of suspicion.

We are not allowed to talk about Subhadra. Mother does not want me to live in the shadow of death. She cannot forget the loss of her own mother and is inconsolable when she returns from Subhadra's house. Granny insists that she rest and gives her a little brandy to calm her down. Mani and Fatima fan her head and press her feet, and mumble something about the death of her mother. Granny says that Mother is not in any condition to take care of me.

My disturbed nights are filled with unanswered questions. Field rats and mongooses run on the roof tiles and green-faced winged ogres, feet turned the wrong way, creep into my nightmares. They hang upside down from the ceiling like bats, and I wake up talking in my sleep.

I need something more than Granny's soft white sari to soothe me. Granny tries to teach me the Shema, which she says will help drive away the evil from my head. I repeat the words which I do not understand. She shows me the mezuzah on the door and says that I have nothing to be afraid of.

Purple faces with horns surface beside the green faces and I see Subhadra. We play a game of nagolchu. With seven stones piled one on top of the other, we try to topple the first stone with a ball which flies over Subhadra's head, and a rope falls from it and makes a noose around her feet. She flies upside down into the sky, the rope carrying her away like the kite in school which snatched my chapati. I snuggle deeper into my quilt with its design of green parrots and red roses.

I must forget the night birds. I need help.

Mani scares me with her interpretations of my dreams. Because I am innocent and Subhadra was so close to me, she is sure that I will see the truth in my dreams.

hanuman

While we sit on the floor and chat, a black-faced male langur baring his shining white teeth and red gums, rushes into the kitchen from the open verandah and snatches a tea-soaked slice of bread from Amina. She screams. She has always been afraid of being bitten by a monkey and the many injections she would have to accommodate in the folds of her stomach.

Mani, always philosophical when calamity descends, fans Amina as she sits panting on the floor with her legs spread out, and tells me that langurs are basically kind creatures and that perhaps they could help me. Amina blows into the saucer of hot tea that Fatima has just offered her and tells me not to listen to Mani. But they all agree that prayers to Hanuman can drive the ghosts away from this mortal world and also help keep away the langurs which scare me so much. Their eyes dart to the doorway to see if Granny or any of the other older women are around and they offer to take me to the temple. But how can I go with them? The family would never allow such madness.

Father comes to pick me up on the cycle. I sit behind him, clinging to his back like a baby monkey and Mani arranges my dress and slips a book of prayers to Hanuman into my school bag. I sleep with the book under my pillow, and pull the bedsheet over my head.

The dreams continue. Subhadra, her hand frozen in the mudra of applying a tilak, seems to have found a permanent place in the oblique sculptures moving in circles in the ceiling of my mind. Her eyes are wide open, and a beatific smile plays on her lips. Eyes of stone look into the palm of her hand, the mirror of her fate.

In the garden, I pretend to read the prayer book although the script will not yield its meaning to me.

I roll lumps of clay to create a Hanuman. Modelling the head of an animal on the body of a man is not easy. My Hanuman is a crumbling mass of clay.

I borrow an earthen lamp and sindoor from Mohun and try to pray to my god with a brass bell. The sound feels good. Mohun does not know my fears, but sits down and prays with me. He then explains to me the danger of making gods with clay and leaving them unguarded under the night sky. He sees the fear in my eyes and suggests that we rectify my error by immersing my god in the lily pond. I ask him to keep the book. He decides to fast for a day in case I have done something wrong. I feel guilty that he suffers for me and the food chokes in my throat.

I do not have to tell Mohun that it is our secret.

Every time I walk past the lily pond, I see the dissolving lump of clay, my little god sitting quietly at the bottom of the pond. If Mohun hadn't known about it, I could have kept my secret to myself for a long time.

But then, under the night sky, the mass of clay would perhaps have taken the form of another ogre and joined my tormentors.

chains

N aomi does not know that I know the story of her mother. Danieldada has told me everything. Not at one stretch, but on different days, at different times, in different moods. But always in the same place, on the swing. I have put the pieces together, and I brood over death—

Subhadra's and my grandmother Leah's—and try to understand the concept of being and not being.

I am afraid of becoming motherless and homeless like the beggar woman. My mother's fresh pink sari has the feel of life. I wish she would hold me more often in her arms.

Danieldada talks softly. The peacocks and parrots on the brass chains listen with me and I keep pace with the rhythm of the swing with my foot, careful not to make a sound in case it disturbs Dada and he stops talking. I know now why Dada looks so sad. Sometimes he opens his steel cupboard with the bad key, the one with the catch that grates jarringly after the second turn, and brings out my anklets. The silver bells tinkle as I unwrap them from the crisp red paper and I know that Dada is in a mood to talk.

As if performing a secret ceremony Danieldada hooks on my anklets. Everything about these afternoons is like eating forbidden fruit. We wait impatiently for the days when we can be alone in the house.

Danieldada is not supposed to tell me all that has happened. Mother has definite ideas about how much I should know about her mother. He says Naomi has warned him that I should never feel the shadow of her sadness. But when one sits with Dada, it is like sitting under a tree with its world of shadows, lights and colours.

He needs to talk to someone. If not me, it would have been the squirrel that comes looking for crumbs on the verandah. He says that he would never tell his story to anyone else but feels that I must know the truth. His secret is like a ghost which lives with him. Every time we are alone his first question is whether I have told anybody his story. He is jealous of my friendship with Cousin Samuel. He does not know that I only listen to Samuel's stories and never tell him mine, not even those about Subhadra.

From Danieldada's stories I have understood better why Mother has never been able to adjust to our other house, which she often calls a village square. She needs to live quietly with the memories of her mother.

I am trying to understand Danieldada's attitude towards Mother. They seem to be uncomfortable with each other and Mother worries constantly about the fact that she is not her father's son. She tries hard to be the man of the family. She goes to work and the two men stay at home. She always seems to carry more domestic responsibilities than they do, but sometimes, she tires of her role and feels relieved when Danieldada depends more on Father. I wonder whether she purposely created a crisis in the other house so that we could move in with my grandfather. I think she wanted to give Dada the son she was not.

between fathers

Father enjoys his new role. Now he is suddenly a man of importance, while in the other house, Uncle Menachem still rules supreme.

I must tell you more about my father. I have come to know him better after we came to live in Danieldada's house.

Like all the men of our family, he is a very good-looking man, whose thick mane of hair and neatly trimmed, imposing moustache contrast with Uncle Menachem's bushy unkempt looks.

Unlike Father, Uncle Menachem never seems to find time for the barber. He is always busy reading medical journals and preparing herbal concoctions for fevers and headaches. He takes great pride in his fez cap of lambskin which he arranges with careful precision on his head. That is the only time he looks at himself in the mirror.

Mirrors fascinate Father. If he could, he would have one in each room, so that he could see himself from various angles and in different places. This annoys Mother who looks at a mirror only when she dabs her face with powder, or arranges the last pin in her bun. She feels that looking at oneself is vanity. But in the matter of mirrors, Father ignores Mother and Danieldada supports him, as he feels a man must know what he looks like.

A nine-inch mirror is Father's mobile vanity trapping. It is moved from the dining table to the bathroom and to the garden on Sundays where it waits for Sulemanbhai. Father's well-groomed looks depend on him. In the garden, near the rose bush, Father sits in the sun with his eyes closed.

In the morning sun, Sulemanbhai's hennaed hair with its yellow streaks matches the colour of the roses. Swept backward without a parting, it contrasts with the white beard bristling under two paan-stained buckteeth. The effect is startling. His brown eyes shine dangerously like a hyena's. He looks as though he might slit Father's throat with his blade. But in reality, he is very loyal to Father. He has been the family barber for four generations. He was present even at Father's circumcision, and had caressed the newborn baby's hair. He knew, even then, that in Father he had a customer for life.

Sulemanbhai lives in a two-room tenement behind Grandmother's house in Delhi Chakla. His plump wife Bilkis makes the most delicious egg pudding. He cycles down to Shahibagh on his red bicycle, carrying an assortment of razors, knives and tweezers in a small green tool box with a design of pink roses. A high-backed chair and two stools wait for him. The tool box is placed on one stool, while he sits on the other, and Father has the chair facing the mirror.

Sulemanbhai spreads a white sheet on Father's bare chest and as he dozes off, sharpens the blade on the whetstone, quickly dips the brush in hot water and makes a lather from a bar of soap pressed into a brass bowl. He applies the lather on Father's cheeks with circular wrist movements as if he were a painter, and then delicately shaves Father's face with the razor blade, leaving the skin smooth and shining. Like a toreador he walks around Father studying his hair, attacking it now and then with sharp-edged scissors. Then he lifts the sheet, now covered with hair, and shakes it in the direction of the rose bush. Sulemanbhai's movements never change. Only his stories vary from funerals to weddings, births to elopements. He knows everything about everybody and loves sharing what he knows with Father in his strange Palanpuri Hindi. Sometimes Father and I find ourselves speaking the same kind of Hindi which is characteristic of Dilhi Darwaza.

Mother feels Sulemanbhai gossips too much and that he
pollutes our Hindi. But Danieldada says that if he did not speak
as much as he did, he would not be able to work. He needs the
sound of his own voice to function with precision. His tongue
falls silent only when he holds the mirror up for Father to see
himself, and he observes closely the reaction to his workmanship.

Father then lifts his arms, so that Sulemanbhai can shave
his chest and underarms. After this Father wakes up fully and
asks Mother to prepare his bath. While brass buckets rattle in
the bathroom, Sulemanbhai concentrates on Father's nails. He
cuts them with a blade, polishes them and cuts the dead skin
around them. It makes me feel funny in my stomach.

I prefer Danieldada's made-in-England nailcutter.

Rifles fascinate Father and so does antique furniture.

Mother worries about Father's future. To avoid arguments at
the dining table, he does not speak about rifles. If he brings
home partridges, which he knows I particularly like, Mohun
quietly cooks them. I wonder how many partridges make a curry
for five? But Dada likes to talk about rifles, birds and antique
furniture and Mother becomes tense while we eat. So Father
answers his questions without looking at Mother, and in much
the same way, Danieldada too avoids her eyes.

Sometimes I wonder whether Dada is a bad influence on
Father.

He is sure that in time Father will make it but Mother is not,
and asks him sarcastically how one can find work with a rifle?
The veins on Father's hands tighten as he picks up a partridge
wing with his chapati. I am worried. Will Father continue to eat

or leave the table ? I do want to lick the brown sauce at the bottom of the pan. I wait for the conversation to turn to lighter topics and sigh with relief when Father chooses the partridge. I wish he'd look as happy as he does when he enters the house with the shikar slung across his shoulder. To me he looks like Tarzan, with his perfect features and beautiful hair.

Danieldada offers the use of his garage to Father. He does not have a car any more and suggests Father set up a workshop to make his own furniture or even to repair guns. The two men seem to believe in each other. Mother is disturbed. She argues with Danieldada whether it would not be safer financially for Father to work in an office as he himself had done. Dada replies that he had the mind of an office worker but Father is different.

If he'd had a son, says Danieldada, he would have encouraged him to do something creative. I wonder why he never helped his daughters cultivate their talents. Yet it is reassuring to feel the bond between the men and the fortress of my city feels stronger.

I always associate the smells of sawdust, gunpowder, tobacco and forests with Father. Hasmukh Mistry, the carpenter he discovered in the river bazaar selling carved coffee tables, works with him. I cannot understand how anyone can smoke so many bidis. His name means 'smiling face', but he never smiles.

The drought in Banaskantha brought him to Ahmedabad and I see the dry cracked earth in his eyes. He was forced to sell his land and has never been able to earn enough to go back to his wife and three children, but he sends them a money order for two hundred rupees every month, although he says it is very difficult for him to do so.

To have a cow and a field gives life meaning, says Mistry. Instead of sleeping under a tree in his field, he sleeps on the footpath under a streetlight. Another man from his village stays with him and they cook their thick bajri rotlas on a clay pan over an open fire.

Hasmukh has a bath under the garden tap and eats in the kitchen with Mohun. But in the evenings he prefers to return to his friend on the Ambavadi footpath. Father now works harder as he feels responsible for Mistry. Together they make coffee tables with carvings. My mother is less tense and more helpful. Father returns to the workshop after dinner to repair guns for nawabs and rajas, and she sits at the dining table writing his accounts.

durga

The mosaic of Danieldada's life emerges from the fire of the afternoon sun beating down on the open verandah. Through the coolness of the reed-mat screen, I can feel the presence of my grandmother Leah. She died when my mother was as old as me.

According to Danieldada, she did not want to live any more as she had lost her trust in him and since then his daughter Naomi, my mother, hates him.

Long ago, says Danieldada, he had sometimes felt the urge to go to the synagogue and had particularly liked Simhath Torah, those occasions when they brought out the Books and danced around the teva. His fingers play with the frayed gold embroidery of his old blue skull cap, as he shows it to me. Eyes twinkling, he tells me that he knew the women liked to watch him.

It was on days like these that he felt more Jewish than ever, with his shoulders touching those of his brethren, his feet moving in rhythm to the beat of an ancient Hebrew chant.

He would return home and expect Leah and their daughters to follow the now forgotten Jewish rituals. It was as if the traditions were a raft he wanted to hold on to, because Leah and he were moving in different directions. She was absorbed in the inner world of the house, while he found himself drifting towards the card table and late night parties at the club.

They hardly spoke to each other any more. Rituals were forgotten, but sometimes Hebrew words would stray into their memories for a fleeting moment.

There was emptiness and in the altar of the mind, there was no image which seemed to fit. Except the nude figurine of Parvati in the glass showcase.

Dada says he was shocked at himself. He wanted to die when he found himself drowning under the surface of his Durga's dark skin and the silver bell of her voice.

While playing a game of badminton at the club, Naomi had seen her father's little card table affair. Danieldada says it had meant nothing to him but Mother had been too young to understand, and had felt threatened.

Leah had spent her days with her mind dulled by the monotonous routine of her home—counting the clothes for the dhobhi who came with a little bullock, telling the cook to wash the coriander leaves, fixing the mosquito nets around the beds and spraying the rooms with insecticide. Later, after washing her face and arranging her long hair in a bun at the nape of the neck, she would sit listening to the cicadas as she waited for the family to return in the evening, sometimes dozing in the cane chair under the jasmine creeper. A grinding routine, but then a comforting one.

Naomi's knowing eyes were soon Leah's eyes.

Her world must have broken apart, the calm routine of her life dissolving in a whirlpool of disturbances. The empty alcove of her mind now had the form of a woman. Durga, dark, beautiful and threatening.

Like most Jewish women of her generation, Leah had been brought up to believe that looks were not important, that women should dress modestly and preserve their virtue. For generations it had been one of the unspoken rules of the elders that Jewish women should be self-effacing; as long as they did not attract attention, the community was not in any danger.

Danieldada was himself attracted to colour and glamour, but expected his daughters to follow the traditional way of life as he did not want them to become susceptible to undesirable influences. Mother also imposes the same rules on me.

Leah had married her second cousin Daniel as a teenager, and they had been like siblings who had had a similar upbringing. Unknown to her daughters, Leah had shared a deep bond with her husband. She had known that he liked to look at beautiful women but had not imagined he would be unfaithful to her. According to Danieldada, Leah must have been disturbed by Mother's description of Durga and it must have hurt her pride to find that her daughter was aware of her father's affair with another woman.

The photograph of Leah reveals a tired body with sagging breasts and eyes innocent of any coquetry. Durga with her large black eyes, narrow waist and firm young body must have swept into Grandmother's dreams in the form of her namesake, with swords in her many hands, sitting astride a tiger.

Mani would have said it was like being haunted by a ghost.

Danieldada was struggling to maintain his balance against the female elements of the universe. He was constantly dusting away the specks of kumkum that fell on his coat from Durga's bindi, and trying to light the Shabbat candles. Comfort to him still meant green-striped pyjamas and speaking Marathi, their mother tongue in exile. It was comparing progress reports, the price of vegetables and sharing family recipes, like the one for the rubbery wheat milk halva. It meant fitting into his role as father and husband rather than that of a man of the world. But he could not resist the lure of the unfamiliar—Hindu festivals, sensuous miniature paintings, rounded hips swaying to the sound of drums, and the colours that flooded the empty altar of his mind. Leah could never recognise him whenever he stepped out

of the house with his fancy walking stick. Yet, it was as if she
were a part of his own flesh and she always took him back into
the circle of her life. She was sister, wife, mother. The familiar.
But she was past her youth and had growing daughters, who
were only a little younger than the women who attracted their
father. She had become insecure, a prey to dark depressing
silences and unexpected furies, and Danieldada suddenly found
himself confronting a Leah he did not know.

At some point, his vision grew so clouded that he could no
longer see the light. He went to live with Durga in the cantonment,
near the Hanuman temple and the British officers' bungalows.
There was a certain ruthless cruelty in his being so close to the
house, and yet so far away from everything.

banyanbaba

L eah's pleas for her husband's return at the dargah of the walking saint went unanswered and she decided to see the one known as Banyanbaba. She thought he would be an old man with long matted hair which looked like the roots of the banyan tree.

I open the doors of my grandmother Leah's silence and see her stepping into another world—from the quiet neighbourhood of Shahibagh near the mansions of the seths and the British army camp with its line of asopalav trees, she enters the heart of the walled city and reaches her destination with apprehension.

The place is not really unfamiliar to her. She grew up in an old three-storeyed house close to the flower bazaar in Phool-gali near the synagogue. She had lived a cloistered life and had never been allowed to play in the busy street edged with pyramids of marigolds, blood-red roses, and green asopalav leaves.

Her parents had led uneventful lives—Leah's father worked in a booking office in the Railways. It was a clockwork existence, lived out between lunch and dinner. I can imagine him clutching his lotus-embroidered shopping bag and pressing the gills of pomfrets at Teen Darwaza, breaking the tails off bhindis to check their freshness, and never accepting bribes, never obliging acquaintances who asked for tickets out of turn and avoiding school friends who took part in the freedom struggle. Shuttered eyes like a closed booking window.

Dada says that Leah's father usually waited for his dinner sitting in a deckchair in the kitchen, reading a Marathi magazine and occasionally instructing his wife on what ingredients to use. Shabbat was religion and he never missed the Friday prayers with the community. He knew prayers for all occasions, though not what they meant. At home, there was a strong awareness of being Jewish, which set them apart from their neighbours. This had been the reason why the beautiful, virtuous and well-brought up Leah of the fair skin and curly hair had been chosen as a bride for her cousin Daniel who was handsome and educated and held a secure job in a British company. In the first years of their life together, Leah had been shocked by her husband's vivacity. She would have preferred to have been the wife of someone quiet and sedate like her own father.

Soon Leah's father was transferred to Bombay where their son had settled and she lost the only friend she had ever had, her mother. Danieldada's parents had also left to live with their older unmarried daughter who was a doctor to the royal family of Radhanpur.

Alone with her husband who did not bother too much about everyday Jewishness and preferred his whisky and cards at the club, Leah slowly found herself losing interest in rituals. Yet she fasted on Yom Kippur, asking forgiveness for all the traditions she did not follow, for mixing milk and meat and for sometimes saying things she should not have said. It had been easier to feel more Jewish near the synagogue.

Lifting her sari to step over the cowdung and lowering her eyes with shame at exposing her calves, Leah stepped beyond the dividing line. She sensed that once she confronted Ravana, things would perhaps get out of hand, as they had for Sita. She was crossing the thin line that had always separated her from things that were not Jewish. She knew she was pushing back the perimeter of her world to include another dimension about which she knew nothing, to go beyond the limits of a life which had extended from the kitchen and the garden to the synagogue, the gymkhana club and the few houses she had been invited to.

Her childhood in the walled city with her mother was like the dry rose petal that she sometimes came across when she opened her small leather-bound autograph book.

Yet, this street seemed to take her back to another age, where the enlightened gave potions that brought back stray husbands, drove ghosts away from heads and houses, cured illnesses and offered hope to barren women. Closed wooden doors, carved bannisters, the old banyan tree in the courtyard, alive with the chirping of the black-headed, pink-feathered rosy pastors; roots hanging like witches' hair from branches; water dripping from the copper pot onto the linga below the tree. Leah's eyes moved away, embarrassed by the phallic symbol.

Leah had written a letter to her mother, but she had not lived to post it. I found it in the long untouched family Bible when I was trying to figure out the difference between Subhadra's gods and mine. Old fragments falling apart like the relationship between Danieldada and my mother. Instinctively I had known that her signature at the end meant that I should ask Dada about the letter and not Mother.

Strange how it became a part of Danieldada's life, lying next to his pillow—written in Marathi, in fading brown ink on old lined paper, in a hand like a little girl's, speaking about her fears. He tells me what the letter is all about and asks himself whether this was reason enough for her to end her life.

The street where my grandmother Leah went to consult the guru remains almost unchanged. The sun never shines there, only brushes the surrounding rooftops and slants into the courtyards. Cyclists weave through the crowded streets ringing their bells. To get to the door one has to squeeze between the cow licking spilt dal on the road and the Rabari milkwomen with brass pots on their heads. Every morning the sweeper woman sweeps the road with her long triangular broom and the smell of milk and cowdung merge into the rhythm of the women washing clothes. Dada says the street looks the same as it did before.

I can see Leah praying at the Chalte Pir ki Dargah every Wednesday as her mother had advised her to. But not seeing any change in her husband, she had turned to Banyanbaba after hearing stories of his miracles from his disciples, Hasina her general help and Shielaben her neighbour.

Hasina's stomachache had been cured by a bottle of holy water and her son had passed his high school examinations after baba had circled his head with seven ripe lemons and thrown them at the crossroads. There were many such stories and they said these potions were harmless, but that the instructions had to be followed to the letter.

The ghodagadi enters a dirty lane that squeezes between two dilapidated houses. At the end of it is a huge wooden door and a wicket gate that opens into a courtyard. The bigger door always remained closed and Leah must have felt trapped. Perhaps she had wished to rush back home and lie down on the cool four-poster bed.

A bearded man sits smoking a clay pipe that emits the strong herbal fragrance of ganja. Sheilaben and Hasina are deep in conversation with him as they all wait for Banyanbaba's darshan. Perhaps Leah no longer wanted to see him, but could not tell the women how she felt since they would have considered it blasphemous to return home without baba's darshan. And anyway, she did not know how to interrupt their intense conversation.

The door opens, and a young widow in a white sari with vibhuti smeared on her forehead beckons them in. The women enter a room redolent with the fragrance of sandalwood agarbattis. It is bare but for a carpet on which the devotees are expected to sit. In a corner a bearded man grinds opium. The windows and doors are closed. A strong sun shines outside. Inside, it is dark. A single yellow bulb shines from under a frilled white ceramic lampshade, and a black pedestal fan placed on the floor whirs slowly, menacingly. Banyanbaba holds court seated on a tiger skin with his eyes closed, a white dhoti tied around his well-fed stomach, his hairy chest bare except for a string of rudraksha beads. The strong smell of agarbattis gives Leah a headache and she wants to run away.

Sheilaben and Hasina kneel in front of the guru and touch their heads to the floor. He blesses them by raising his palm and Leah tries to imitate her friends, but feels paralysed with fear. Anyway with her bad knee she could not have accomplished the feat as easily as the other two.

Contrary to what Leah had imagined Banyanbaba does not have a beard, and he is bald. On his forehead shines a huge circle of kumkum, and his thick lips are stretched in a permanent half-suppressed smile. Something about him reminds her of the stuffed tiger's head.

Piercing eyes read Leah's thoughts and to her shock the guru asks her in English for the details of her problem. The tension eases. Leah tells the story of her husband to a total stranger, and ends up feeling confused and relieved.

The man listens with closed eyes, lips moving in a chant, his head transformed from the tiger's head to a Buddha's, like the one that sits atop her radio at home. But this man's fist is closed, unlike the Buddha's. His eyes open and a rupee with the inscription of King George's profile appears in the soft bed of his palm. Hasina and Sheilaben look at Leah with expressions that say 'didn't I tell you'. Later that night they would regale an audience of awestruck women with stories of the guru and all that they had seen with their own eyes.

The coin should be placed under her husband's pillow, he says, and asks Leah to bend her head so that he may tie a black thread to ward off the evil eye of jealous people. A chill runs down Leah's back as the fat hand seems to touch the skin of her neck. But his face is expressionless as he asks her to donate fifty rupees and she begins to think it is almost like going to a doctor. She places the money at his feet, feeling embarrassed under his watchful gaze.

He impresses Sheilaben and Hasina by calling her madam, and blessing her : 'Go, the mother is with you,' while all Leah really wanted was her own mother.

She waited till Danieldada came back home for a few days and slipped the coin with the kumkum stain under the pillow, always removing it before he woke up.

But there was no change. As long as he stayed with them, he seemed to come home later than usual, and there were never any reasons given. If she questioned him, he flew into a rage. The daughters heard his rantings with tears drenching their

pillows, so terrified were they that their father would leave for
the other house the next morning and never return. It was as if
they were always on the edge of a precipice.

amavas

 mavas. 'These moonless nights are bad,' said Sheilaben. 'It is then that the evil spirits are at work.'

One day after amavas, Leah remembered that she had left the bed without removing the coin. Whenever he was there, she and Danieldada always had their

morning tea together on the verandah. But that day when she
stepped out with the tray, she almost dropped it when she saw
him tossing the coin in the air.

The shoe-shine boy was polishing his shoes, a ritual
Danieldada liked to supervise himself, and Leah stood by
helplessly watching him toss the coin at the boy and say that he
did not like colour on his coins. The boy was pleased to have a
month's salary in advance and caught the coin as he would have
a cricket ball.

As if that were not enough, Danieldada suddenly noticed the
black thread around Leah's neck and even before she could place
the cup on the table, he had pulled away the string and thrown it
into the ashtray, asking her if she was ill and should he call the
doctor. He knew the maid Hasina sometimes persuaded Leah to
wear black strings for her headaches which she was certain were
the effect of someone's evil eye. The day had begun badly for
Leah. When he went for a bath she picked up the thread and hid
it in her blouse. She had to see the guru; she was afraid of his
goddess and her wrath.

That afternoon Hasina had her day off and Sheilaben had
decided to make her yearly quota of urad dal papads. So Leah
braced herself to meet the guru alone. He repeated the word
'misfortune' several times and put his palm on her thigh in the
presence of the widow. Leah must have seen the lust in his eyes
and felt the perspiration on his palm seeping through her sari.
She must have been afraid that the bearded man would lock the
door and trap her in with the guru, and rushed out thinking that
neither her husband nor the guru were what they appeared to
be.

In her eyes they both wore the tiger's skin.

In the guru's eyes she would have seen something she herself had not dared to look at properly, her own naked body, lying on the duree, pinned to the floor by the widow and the bearded man, just like the pictures in the books which Danieldada kept hidden under his clothes.

At the guru's place she must have eaten the prasad and allowed his disciples to apply the sindoor on her forehead. In her determination to get her husband back, she must have burned with strange fires. Ceremonies with kumkum powder, fire and ghee frightened her. She rolled the sweet into a ball in her palms and slid it into her handkerchief, and when she returned home, she washed the sindoor from her forehead as if it were blood. She hated her husband for enjoying the rituals that scared her.

Danieldada was amazed that Leah had gone to consult the guru. Years after her death, he would remember the matter of the coin and curse himself for not having paid any attention to it. He had seen the thread lying coiled like an asp in the ashtray, but when he had returned from his bath it had not been there, and she had not reacted when she heard him inform the cook that he would not return for dinner. He had not realised that the string lay curled up in Leah's blouse and she was waiting to seek the guru's advice. The moonless night and the happenings of the next day must have suffocated Leah.

He thinks that she must have gone by the ghodagadi up to the Ellis bridge near Bhadra fort to throw the string into the river since she knew that all holy things, whether one believed in them or not, had to be thrown into the river. She must have then returned home utterly disillusioned with her husband and with men in general. The coin and the thread had not been effective.

Danieldada feels that none of this would have happened had she expressed her feelings strongly enough or if they had tackled their problems by quarrelling with each other like his friends, Bharucha and his wife Zenobia. Although Leah had seemed to have accepted his lifestyle, what she had done proved that she had not. She had never known how to protest.

Danieldada says that Leah's eyes rarely betrayed emotion—after all, generations of mothers had taught their daughters to preserve themselves for their future Jewish grooms by not showing what they felt—and so he had searched for it elsewhere. But Leah's last emotion, powerful enough to make her commit suicide, had shaken him. He knew he had failed both himself and her by not understanding her better.

In his hunger for excitement and romance he had lost something invaluable. Although he had allowed himself to be totally bewitched by Durga, he could not imagine life without Leah. Selfishly, he had wanted them both.

Leah had never been touched by any male except Danieldada, and her father and brothers when they'd kissed her occasionally on her cheeks and it had taken many years and the birth of three daughters before she could endure her husband's touch without feeling a sense of sin.

She must have been very disturbed about the guru touching her for there must have been something in his eyes, as if he had commanded her to shake her hair loose and lower her sari.

Danieldada had wanted Leah to be comfortable at the parties he was often invited to. He thought she would look beautiful in a dress, and had asked Zenobia to stitch her a special one, pale mauve with silver sequins.

Leah must have been convinced that he would never return. Life, dry as the Sabarmati in summer, must have frightened her. That evening she had sent him a letter through the cook, asking him to think of the family. He had angrily replied that he did not like to receive letters at the club. When he had seen the cook again at the club, something in the man's face had stopped him from speaking. He had brought news of Leah's death.

Danieldada had found the mauve dress on the bed and a candle-stand on the table. It was as though Leah had tried to hold on to the pleasures of life and religion. She must have returned from the guru's house with feelings of disgust and revulsion, contemplating men and their deceit and her own foolishness in trusting the guru. Her reflection in the mirror must have taunted her. The wetness of her towel showed that she had taken a bath to remove the stains from her thoughts. She must have felt a certain hatred for life. With the dress she must have tried to find a new self that would be a part of her husband's life, and by lighting the candles and saying the 'Shema Israel', she had also tried to hold on to the raft of Jewishness. Danieldada was her raft and he had betrayed her.

He was in the club studying the cards on the table and Leah was lying dead at home. She had burnt herself, making her own ceremony of fire. When he rushed back home, he found Naomi sitting still beside her mother's body. Ever since, she always looked at her father as though she were looking at her mother's burnt face. She absolved herself of the guilt of having told her mother about Durga, crushing out any such thought as if she were crushing a snake's head to make it spit out the venom. But the venom must have entered her system and stayed there, veiled in a scaly skin of false smiles. She must have heard her mother's screams and seen the neighbours trying to break open the door. There are no scars on the door. But there are scars in my mother's eyes and in Danieldada's life. After her death, so shaken was he that his life became like the Day of Atonement.

The shadow of grandmother Leah's face falls on my life.

a love story

Perhaps Samuel is attracted to me. 'You could have been my wife,' he says and in his face that looks like mine, I see the resemblance to our mothers who had both married cousins. 'But now,' sighs Samuel, 'it is impossible. You should go to Israel to look for a groom.'

It is impossible because Uncle Menachem is against intermarriage and speaks about the genetic effects of inbreeding. Madness, stomach problems and cancer, he clucks like an old hen. We look at ourselves in the mirror and wonder which of these illnesses we will get. We all think too much.

I think it would be very easy to be Samuel's wife. We agree about everything and he likes to tell me all about himself, his thoughts, his fears. But I worry that we could end up being as unhappy as Danieldada and Grandma Leah, so familiar to each other and so boring. Will I turn out to be like Mother or Aunty Hannah or Granny or Leah, I wonder.

Perhaps, I will be like the brass Parvati in the showcase. At least, I know I have a body like hers, although Mother always keeps an eye on me and makes sure I never look at myself properly. I try to imitate Parvati—eyelids drooping with unknown desires, lips curved in a secretive smile that Samuel can never understand.

He and I share the same background. We could go on like this forever but the family decides we are brother and sister, and we must find our partners elsewhere although no one knows where. They only know that the partners must be Jewish.

Life is difficult for Malkha: the elders disapprove of her love for Joel and her privacy has been invaded. She is in tears and Uncle Menachem is furious; he feels Joel's brains are in his muscles. He cannot imagine a daughter of the house married to a semi-literate who is likely to end up as a mill worker. He feels Malkha has been raped by a piece of paper.

But Granny secretly approves of Malkha's choice. After all, Joel is her nephew. She thinks it is safer that she looks at Jewish boys. She dreads to think of what would have happened had Malkha been attracted to Anwar's son or to any of the other boys whose windows face the direction of our house. Nobody listens to Granny when she tries to justify the tradition of cousin-marriages. It is difficult to see what lies ahead.

Late into the night the elders hold consultations after the servants go to bed. 'Servants should never know our problems or else the whole street will know. Walls have ears,' says Granny. The family should not get a bad name because of a child, specially a daughter.

Malkha tells me that they've found out about the letters she has been exchanging with Joel, and suspect Fatima of having been the go-between as she works in both the houses. Granny scolds Fatima and tells her that Uncle Menachem does not want her to continue working for us. Fatima cries and asks how a hunchback like her, who has been abandoned by her husband, can survive without working in our house. Aunty Hannah pounces on her and blames her for corrupting a daughter of the house and says she must go.

Fatima grovels on the floor and asks for forgiveness, clutching at Aunty's feet and cursing her own illiterate eyes. She says she thought the pieces of paper she was given were school lessons. Tears stain her patchy grey skin as she moans that had she been educated she would not have been on the streets, thrown out by a husband who could not love her imperfect body.

The matter ends with Aunty Hannah telling Malkha that she is too young to think about such things and Fatima continues to stay with them. I am only two years younger than Malkha and I know I can never dream of being my cousin Samuel's wife. We know everything about each other, but now it is clear that we have to discover another kind of life, about which we do not know anything.

On a Rakshabandhan day in August, under a crescent moon, I tie an orange cotton rakhi on Samuel's wrist. He is now my brother and he places a rupee in my palm as protection money. Aunty Hannah is relieved.

We are not told, nor do we know anything. We may never know anything and nobody wants to help us, perhaps because they themselves know nothing. But we realise that if we do not marry, it is understood that we, the daughters, must live with our aging parents and become their walking sticks. For this, we must educate ourselves. The family seems to be losing faith in the boys. There are more rules for us than there are for them. It is clear that the boys will go away and the girls will stay on. They do not want to lose the girls, because we would never dare to go against them as the boys might. The girls must be preserved for the house.

hindi pikchur

Malkha has diverted her thoughts to more interesting things, like Hindi films. She is always reading film magazines and spends hours in front of the mirror. Aunty tries to keep her occupied by taking her to whichever film she fancies and we all go along with them. We take a ride through the arches of Teen Darwaza towards Central Cinema in the family victoria.

The men prefer to go alone to the morning shows of English films, but sometimes ask the women to dress us up early and take us to a Shirley Temple movie.

We love the glamour of the Hindi cinema—the huge glittering posters of the stars, the handsome heroes brandishing swords, red-lipped heroines in tight bodices and flaring skirts, and the love songs with the bees sitting on flowers. Malkha stands in front of the full-length mirror in the children's room upstairs, biting her lower lip like the heroine we saw last week. She shakes her left hip provocatively, waves her hands above her head and Samuel drums on his desk, hair falling on his forehead.

She has decided to become a film star, and spends hours imagining herself in a multicoloured Rajasthani ghaghra. She dare not ask Aunty Hannah to buy her something so pagan that reveals the little dot of the navel. Malkha imagines herself dancing in a ghaghra and says that when she has all the money in the world, she will buy one. For us, money is freedom, though I doubt if we are ever going to know the meaning of freedom. We do exactly as we are told. We never seem to be able to do all that we want to. And what do we want ? I do not know. It appears there are gates of iron in our walled city and we shall never be able to open them. The iron chain on the door locks us inside the house of our destiny and we can't open the door and walk out for we are welded to the chains. The road outside the door resembles the palm of my hand and I find paths on the lines that frighten Uncle. He seems to see more than any of us.

Like Malkha, I also long for a ghaghra and even think of
asking Danieldada to help me get one. Perhaps I could share it
with Malkha when she comes to spend the day at our house in
Shahibagh and he could take a photograph of us with his camera.

Malkha seems to appreciate my concern for her dreams. One
Thursday, when she spends the day in our house, I wrap Mother's
newly-ironed, coloured saris around our waists. Covering our
heads we tuck the ends into our little breasts just like our
favourite actress, using even Grandmother Leah's blue silk sari.
Dada is thrilled and takes our photographs.

Afterwards, we struggle in vain to fold Mother's saris before
she returns from work. Malkha returns to Dilhi Darwaza in a
hurry for she is tired of being scolded by her elders. My heart
beats wildly as Mother returns and I suffocate in the knots of
the saris. We have encroached upon her privacy and she flies
into a fury, as never before. The blood freezes in my knuckles as
they are rapped, and she screams about the ruined wash. I hate
the yards of memories that knot in my stomach, killing my dream.

Dada tries to save me from Mother's anger, but she is like
Kali on a rampage. I do not know how anyone can stop her. I
somehow realise that her outburst is not just about her saris;
something else erupted in her when she entered the house and
saw me trying to fold her mother's sari, giggling and stepping
on it and almost tearing the old silk. I had disturbed the purity
and sanctity of the dead by mixing them up with the desires of
the living.

The ox tongues are roasting on the coal. One must not dream.

Mani has come to stay with us. Aunty Hannah and Granny
suspect Mani of having stolen a gold ring that had been left in

the bathroom. I feel more settled in her warmth. But she yearns to go back to the old house and waits for the day Hannahbai finds the ring, so that she can return with her head held high.

This is a source of tension between Mother and Aunty, who thinks that Mother is keeping Mani to spite her. When Aunty spends an afternoon with us, she accepts a glass of water from Mani with eyes averted.

Under the canopy of Daryakhan Ghummat, the mosque which looks like a stone tent, the mullah tries to locate the lost ring for Mani.

Mother is obsessed with the fear of losing me and Mani is always with me when I cross roads or visit Granny in a ghodagadi. When I am invited to birthday parties, she waits for me on the pavement outside the house and is always there to watch over me while I play with the neighbours' daughters. I am embarrassed and Mother explains it is because I have grown up.

Together they make a wall around me as though they are guarding me against death. The colour of death is the colour of blood. I feel anger stirring in me and raising its dark hood. In the big house where we were all together and I was the youngest child in a house full of grown-ups, we did not lose our sense of freedom when someone kept an eye on us. But ever since we came to live with Danieldada I feel stifled by the clouds of discord that hover over us. I feel as if I am in a glass case. Mani agrees with Mother's views on bringing up daughters and the only sympathy she offers is a sigh which ends in a half sentence about 'the life of women...'

nail polish and
the nymph

Mother is famous for her guava jam, and feels disturbed that the guava tree behind the house is dying. Mani says, 'The white ants have poisoned our house and they will grow like creepers, spreading under the layers of our lives, always groping for more place, as if they are blind and don't know where they are going.' Mother says I have hair like that, growing everywhere on my head, unruly and wild, and she has to beat it down.

She cannot forgive me because Dada loves me and only tolerates her; and then, there is my hair, which is like her mother's. I find it very strange that Grandmother Leah lives through my hair and sometimes when I sit in the sun drying it, Danieldada touches it and says, 'Thou hast doves' eyes within thy locks.'

I like it without oil, flying around my face. It makes me think of Botticelli's painting of Venus which I saw in one of the art books that Father bought from the river bed market. But it is without oil only on Sundays, when mother washes it with homemade shampoo. I inspect the shape of my fingers, then bite my nails, brown with soapnut powder at the tips.

My nails are chipped and shapeless and have a sour-cream taste. I would like to have long, sharp nails, painted a bright red like the film heroines . At school, Sister Josephina annoys me in the moral science class by saying that women paint their nails to hide the dirt. They should be washed clean and sparkle like pearls in their natural beauty. I disagree, yet shake my head in agreement like everybody else and my friend Pratibha hides her painted nails in shame.

Mother hates nail polish. It is the symbol of the woman who killed her mother, and in her mind, she is dressed in a green chiffon sari and wears red nail polish and lipstick. There is an unspoken taboo against the things I want to experiment with. Pratibha says I must paint my nails if I want to, even if Mother does not like it and that means I must rebel against Mother.

I am obsessed with my nails and in my dreams I walk through a forest of tall bottles of nail polish. Sometimes in Pratibha's house I smell the delicious pink bottle and touch the smoothness of the glass.

She says we could paint just one little fingernail and it is difficult to resist her. We paint a single nail and then I implore her to do all the others. It is like drinking bhang. I am swimming in a lake of nail polish and it is such bliss to hold my nails against the light and see them glow. Pratibha is certain that the colour is pale and that Mother will not notice it.

But Mother has sharp eyes and a nose that smells everything. The mutton is boiling in a black pepper sauce and she is singing a Marathi song while frying puris in the kitchen. As I pick up a steaming hot puri she glances at me. Her hand freezes in mid air and I burn my lips as I try to walk out of the room hiding my hands. I think she is going to brand me with the hot ladle like Subhadra's mother used to. Instead she carefully puts it down, calls me back and reaches for my hands. She studies my nails and her eyes harden as they look into mine. Slowly she asks me for an explanation.

I see the shock in Mother's eyes and instead of crying, I scream.

This is my first act of rebellion.

The second act of rebellion occurs when I break the ritual of having quick baths that must have been passed on for generations from mother to daughter. A chain of mothers whispering to daughters, telling them not to look at their bodies.

The bathroom is our private torture chamber and a perfect setting for murder. As I sit on the low bath stool on the white tiled floor opposite the tap with the bucket of hot water under it, Mother stands over me, rubbing lemon on my neck to lighten the colour of my skin. She would like my neck to be fair, like Malkha's. It irritates her that Hannahbai's daughter should have a fairer complexion.

Mother insists on giving me a bath, as she believes that I will not wash myself properly on my own . But there is also something else; she does not want me to have enough time to look at myself. Under the cover of the lotas of water that she pours over my body, I catch glimpses of a woman I do not recognize. She expects me to remain a child forever and I am fighting against Mother to know myself.

On Sunday mornings, she rubs warm coconut oil into my scalp. I resist and she holds my hair in her fist to keep my head in place, while the soapnut mixture boils on the stove. This is not a serene portrait of mother and child but an act of violence against the flow of my unruly hair. I want to sneeze. My nose runs and I feel the beginnings of a headache. I am allergic to the coconut oil but Mother is convinced that I am putting on an act. The oil soaks into my hair for an hour and then she washes it off with soapnut powder and warm water. As I sit on the bath stool, she soaps me, smiles and says, 'Quick, quick.'

One particular Sunday, I scream at her and tell her to go away. As I snatch the lota from her hand, she loses her balance and slips on the oily floor. I have no sympathy for her. I do not help her and she cries as she heaves herself up with the support of the stool, then opens the door and rushes out. Father, disturbed in the middle of his haircut, asks her to leave me alone.

For the first time I am alone with my body. I let the water flow over me and I am a nymph under the waterfall. I am the rose of Sharon, and the lily of the valley. I take the bar of hard soap and rub it into my scalp, till it feels inflamed and dry. I feel the tears deep down within me.

Outside the bathroom door Mother's anger and sorrow twist my heart as she limps around. All through lunch, she cries and Father orders me 'not to look like that'.

The matter of the hair is over. Father has set me free to have a bath on my own, but nail polish is still taboo. I have been reprimanded by both men who removed all signs of colour from my nails with white spirit from the workshop. Good Jewish girls do not look like 'that'. I am told beauty is purity and comes from within. It sounds dull in the face of colour.

I feel cheated by Danieldada changing sides so easily.

vrindavan

other does not like my being friendly with Pratibha for various unspoken reasons.

Pratibha gives me a lift in her car when I miss the school bus and I like to spend time in her house for she is like an incarnation of Subhadra. Her father has a cloth mill and her house is a mansion. She comes to school in a chauffeur-driven Ford; she eats her lunch with me and gives her Gujarati snacks in exchange for Mother's biscuits and cakes. I have refused to carry old chapatis to school.

Her parents and uncles have separate rooms and it is all very different from Subhadra's house where there was only one room for all nine of them.

I sleep in my parents' room.

Pratibha plays the sitar and her cousin Vatsala learns Bharatnatyam. At home, I throw tantrums. I too want to dance.

Vatsala is amazed at how easily I learn the steps from her. Together we choreograph our own compositions and try to remember all the dances we have seen in films. We have enchanted Sunday afternoons when the shades are drawn and Pratibha beats out the taal on her study table and sings a bhajan as we dance. Mother has never found out why I insist on wearing my only embroidered ghaghra on Sunday afternoons. Vatsala wears a silk one while mine is hand-spun khadi. She lends me a silver bindi shaped like a mango with a little bell in the middle and I always remember to return it to her.

When she finds a peacock feather in the garden, she tucks it in her hair and drapes her mother's sari around her like a dhoti. We dance together and she stands with her right leg crossed over her left, just like the Krishna in the poster in her kitchen and pretends to play the flute while I, Radha the milkmaid, implore him not to bewitch me with his music. He teases me by pulling my sari, I lose my balance and let fall the pot of cream that I am carrying on my head.

When I return home from my sojourn in Vrindavan, everything feels different. Mother in her stiff starched sari is working on some files, Danieldada is listening to the BBC, and Father is polishing a table. I am told to finish my homework.

They do not know of my secret 'Raas Lila'.

I open my geometry notebook and draw pictures of Krishna. He has an attractive oval face with long, heavy lids drooping over his lotus eyes as he plays on the flute held between his curved lips, smiling mysteriously, just like Raphael.

I feel for Raphael what Radha feels for Krishna. He plays the flute and is Samuel's friend. I saw him at the school fun fair where he was in the school band wearing a tie, blue as Krishna's peacock feather. Samuel says he is a Baghdadi Jew and Malkha, noticing the flicker of interest in my eyes, nudges me and giggles.

He is tall and handsome, like the heroes in the Mills and Boon romances which Malkha and I exchange hidden in our school books. But he is not dark like Krishna. He is fair and couldn't possibly like me.

Malkha says boys prefer fair-skinned girls.

I rub orange peel on my skin and give myself a facial, following Granny's recipe of chana ata, rose water, almond paste and fresh cream. I am sure I will catch his eye at the synagogue, and I do. He looks for me in the women's gallery upstairs, and smiles.

Amidst the Hebrew intonations of the congregation, I murmur a Krishna song under my breath, beseeching him not to tease me. Granny smiles at me appreciatively. She does not know what I am saying or she would surely disown me.

Back home in my room, the Hindi film songs from the hit parade on Radio Ceylon fill my ears and tears run down my cheeks. '...king of my dreams, when will I see you...,' I sing softly to myself and dream of Raphael while my school books lie unopened on the table.

broken glass

Mother wants to know everything : what I do in school, how I spend my afternoons in Pratibha's house and all that Danieldada and Father tell me. I do not want to confide in her for the questions in her eyes frighten me. She looks at me as though she suspects I am hiding something, and she is right. I do not think she is being fair with me because if I ask her similar questions, she gets angry. I cannot enter the territory of adults but my life is a thoroughfare. I make up stories that make her laugh. However, the tension tells on me and I dodge Mother by making up excuses and slipping away.

I find it painful, because I know that she told her mother everything and still lost her. Yet she wants me to keep her informed. I am afraid and hope Father will not tell me anything that I would be forced to tell her. She seems to have pushed the guilt over her mother's death to the back of her mind and I am aware of the fact that she must never know that Danieldada has told me everything. It is a make-believe world that encircles Mother and me. She does not know that I lie, often hiding what I should tell her. Sometimes it is difficult as worries and fears find expression on the tip of my tongue and then disappear.

Parties scare me and I never know what to do with my legs and hands, which become like the disjointed limbs of a puppet. At Jenny's birthday party, my out-of-fashion skirt hangs over my knees and makes it very difficult for me to feel comfortable. I worry even if someone comes close enough to speak to me. So I hide behind Mother or Father.

Danieldada has been teaching me to use a fork and at Jenny's party I decide to use it and do so correctly. Suddenly I am not jealous of Jenny or anyone else and my hands and legs no longer feel awkward.

Till we came to live in Shahibagh, I had never been to a birthday party. Our birthdays in Dilhi Darwaza were celebrated with chicken curry, puris, coconut rice and a crate of whisky for Uncle's and Father's friends. We wore new clothes and Granny gave us a silver coin and a hundred rupee note, which our parents quickly took from us saying, 'Children should not carry money.' And instead of cake Granny always ordered king-sized jalebis, decorated with rose petals and dripping with syrup. Mother has promised me a birthday cake, the thought of which makes me nervous. I do not have the courage to tell her that I prefer Granny's ways.

I am preoccupied with my own thoughts when we return home after Jenny's party and I cannot recount to Mother all that Jenny's mother had said to Father. She is suspicious of her and had felt irritated with the woman's constant cries of, 'My! Isn't your husband handsome!' She had been at the other end of the room and in my victory over the fork, I had not paid attention to anything else. Misunderstanding my silence she raises her hand to slap me.

I run, barefoot and angry, away from the house and onto the road. I do not know where…till I see my bloodstained footprints. I have cut my heel on broken glass.

On her way back from the bidi shop Mani finds me huddled on a bench. I beg her not to tell Mother anything. Crying, she carries me to the empty workshop and dresses my wound. She keeps repeating that it is serious and Mother should be told. When Mother suddenly materializes in the doorway, we are both frightened.

Later as I lie in bed with my bandaged foot, I can hear Mother telling Father what a headstrong child I am. She does not tell him the truth and I whisper to myself that I must escape from Mother.

I wonder if a piece of glass will always be waiting to cut my foot.

apsara

When I see my face in Pratibha's god, she says it is a sin. Human beings are not only inferior, but also make mistakes. Gods are perfect in body and in virtue. They live on a higher plane called swarg, where there are no ugly sights and in Indra's court with its divine musicians, gandharvas and dancing apsaras, there is always music in the air.

Pratibha is very patient and is not offended when I ask her if someone like the Dariapur beggar woman would be allowed to enter the court of Indra. She is very clear in her opinion, 'Whether it is an apsara who sins in heaven or common people who sin on earth, they all have to repent and suffer mortal pain. So one must live a good, clean life.'

I hope Subhadra has a safe place in swarg and does not wrong the gods. She is young, innocent and ignorant and may not know what she is doing. I would hate to see her back in Ahmedabad as the little girl on the tightrope. If that were to happen she would not know how to live all over again. It would be better for her to dance to the tune of the gods.

I cannot imagine the leper woman as an apsara and Pratibha sees the questions in my eyes. But she has no more answers, so she asks me whether my god is in the image of human beings. I tell Pratibha that He has a long beard and lives in the sky, that He created the world and I bite my nails with guilt. Uncle Menachem had once told me that He has no form. So I quickly add that He has no form, but you can visualise Him as a grandfatherly figure or a sadhu with a beard.

She tries to help by asking if my god resembles Brahma? I am confused. I am not sure what he looks like, so I quickly say that he must be closer to the prophet Abraham because the name sounds similar.

Suddenly I feel a terrible fear, now that I have sinned by lying about God. I would hate to be dumped at the Dariapur bus-stand as a beggar. I decide it is time to have a conference with Samuel.

But it is no longer easy to speak to Samuel. He has fine hair on his upper lip and on Aunty Hannah's instructions he keeps his distance from me. Yet, when we are alone in Uncle's clinic where he practises the violin, he pulls my plaits and teases me about Raphael. Then, suddenly, his mood changes and he dares me to think about anybody but himself. My heart flutters and I want to ask him if he loves me, but I cannot.

He is jealous because I like Raphael. Yet he wants to know everything about Vatsala. He had spent an afternoon playing cards with us and I think he has been dreaming about her ever since. She is tall and slim with the longest plaits and the tiniest ankles he has ever seen. She has an alluring mole on her left cheek, which had kept his eyes glued to her face. Pratibha in comparison is small and dark but she had looked at him with more interest than Vatsala.

Samuel has no real answers when I question him about our God. He now wears spectacles and affects the style of a professor, often removing them and wiping the glass. They make him look very intelligent. He puts them on, smiles and says, 'God is Love.'

Granny says if I want to ask questions I must visit on Friday, for Shabbat, when Uncle Menachem has time to answer them.

I cannot go because Mother says nobody is free to take me to Dilhi Darwaza, and I am not allowed to travel alone by bus. I feel trapped and dream about the Shabbat candles on Granny's dining table. I wish I were Malkha's sister.

Mother does not light the Shabbat candles. She says, 'Work is God.'

I ask Mani. For her, the concept of Allah is clear. He exists in her heart, and though she does not know what he looks like, he is everywhere. She thinks about my problem and comes up with the solution that when one is confused, God exists in the eyes of one's parents. That is why, she says, Pratibha and Vatsala take their parents' blessings by touching their feet. It is like touching the feet of the gods. It is the same with teachers and saints. She is convinced that if I tried hard I could perhaps see God in people. But she has no answers when I ask her about the black stone of Kaaba and is rather shocked when I tell her that the picture of it in her bag resembles a Shivalinga. She looks shocked and says, 'Baby, you are mad.'

Father says he has never thought about God. He does not feel the need to do so. He feels Jewish and that is enough for him. I swallow the words: but what about me ? 'Love,' he continues, 'is God.' I wish he would understand my simple question about the image of God. He, who knows how to fashion forms in wood, should be able to explain this but he cannot. Instead he tells me, 'I felt the presence of God when I met your mother, and on the day you were born.' His eyes move from the parrot he is carving and rest on me with affection.

I do not know how to react for I have never seen that look in the Dilhi Darwaza house.

I resign myself to my fate.

between pleats

Mother is an unusual woman. She tells me that love was the emotion she experienced when she saw Father for the first time and it was she who proposed to him. In a Jewish community where the unions are between families and not those actually concerned, that must have been an act of rebellion. I have never seen Mother in such a good mood.

On their fourteenth wedding anniversary she tells me the story of her marriage to Father. Granny has organized a family get-together and we are dressing up for the occasion. She is helping me to wear a sari and has surprised me by offering her yellow silk one with the peacock border. It is one of the saris I had crumpled in my desire to make a skirt for Malkha and I can't wait to see Malkha's face turn green. I am sure Aunty Hannah will insist on her wearing the pink-sequined dress with the funny frills she hates so much and I am also sure she will be embarrassed and annoyed because Joel will be there and she would like so much to show him her fair waist.

I tell my mother I want to wear the sari the way she does. Despite the fact that she never shows any part of her body, I must say she is a very well-dressed woman, unlike the others at the synagogue or at her office. Her pastel-coloured saris are heavily starched and she arranges each pleat neatly, one over the other, making perfect creases with her hands. When she comes back from work her hair and sari look as neat, as if she were leaving home instead of returning to it. She always looks fresh.

Aunty Hannah, on the other hand, does not bother which part of her body is exposed. Her breasts can be seen, either through the sari or below her low neckline, and her back and waist are always visible. Her saris are more expensive, yet it is Mother who looks smarter. It must be because Mother works and Aunty stays at home and in some ways I am sure they are both jealous of each other.

Between pleats, pins, and adjusting the length of the pallav, Mother tells me the story of her love for Father. She saw him at the typing institute which she attended after her graduation. The institute was run by one of Father's more enterprising friends whom he visited whenever he had the time to spare. Mother had decided to find work to become independent. Her sisters had found the easy way out, eloping even while they were in their teens, which in reality must have been difficult.

The subject is taboo in our house. Julie married Iqbal in a Muslim ceremony and now lives in Delhi. She was renamed Julekha and once a year there is a card from her for Id and Danieldada collects them in a brown paper bag in his cupboard. 'Insha Allah,' he says, 'it is good she is alive.' His favourite, his youngest daughter Sinora went through a church wedding with their neighbour Peter. Dada had been heartbroken because she had not invited him for the ceremony. But she made up for it by writing long letters about her life in Bombay, and sending photographs of her children and in-laws. They are consigned to a plastic bag, next to the brown-paper one.

When I am older I will ask Danieldada about his guilt and his opinion on marriage. When I look at the faded photograph of the three sisters whom I resemble vaguely, I panic.

Mother knew Father was the man she was looking for—reserved, handsome and Jewish. He must have been attracted by Mother's simplicity, but he had not been ready to take a wife.

When she had invited him for tea, he had gladly agreed. It was the first time a woman had invited him to her house. She was unlike anyone he had known and I am sure he was shocked, curious and flattered.

Her house contrasted sharply with his own. Her pearl pink sari, the embroidered tablecloth with the matching plates against a backdrop of lace curtains; all this, along with his favourite semolina laddus and mince-cutlets, must have seemed like a perfect way to begin a romance.

Mother had learnt to make her own decisions and look after herself after Grandmother Leah's tragic death. She was even willing to adapt to the 'not-so-sophisticated' house at Dilhi Darwaza. Her father obviously had 'no face' to approach any other Jewish family for an alliance. With Leah dead, he could not keep their home together and none of them could pick up the pieces.

In the small and orthodox community where the elders were the matchmakers and took all the major decisions, Mother broke all convention when she proposed to Father who, no doubt, would have preferred a traditional proposal, one sent by his family to her father. Danieldada too says that Mother embarrassed him by behaving the way she did. She did not want Danieldada to approach Father's family with the proposal in case they humiliated him because of his past and insisted that Father himself should break the news to his family. Danieldada would have preferred it if Mother had remained unmarried and looked after him. It was then that I realised why he had a strained relationship with Mother.

He still remembers the day Mother decided to tell him about her decision. It was heartening for him because unlike her sisters she had not eloped. But she had chosen an inopportune moment. He was sitting at the dining table, looking into a small mirror and cutting the hair on his ears with a sharp pair of scissors, listening to the English news on the radio about the deportation of Jews. Naomi's words had cut through him like a knife. He remembers that tears had rolled down his cheeks and that his hand had trembled. His daughter had held him so that he would not hurt himself.

Granny also didn't approve of Mother breaking convention and was not at all sure if she wanted an independent and educated daughter-in-law, but told herself that it was better than Father bringing home a girl from another community. It was Uncle Menachem who supported Mother and admired her boldness, much to Aunty Hannah's displeasure. He said he would welcome a bride who had a mind of her own. Granny reconciled herself to Naomi's proposal by pretending ignorance and came to meet Danieldada to ask formally for Naomi's hand.

At family dinners she liked to make Mother blush with the story of my parents' romance, describing the episode in Marathi and mimicking Father's shy answer to Mother's sharp, 'Will you marry me?'

Those were happy days when Granny made us laugh, stuffing us with modaks, steamed with coconut and raisin filling and Samuel used to weave a string of chrysanthemums for my hair, just like Krishna. Our eyes would melt with love and I can still hear him whispering, 'Sister, will you marry me?'

We belong to the womb of our family. My sari sweeps the floor and we doze together in the smoothness of silk.

the shipwreck

Father says Danieldada is very ill. An incurable ulcer has ruined his stomach and dinnertime is no longer fun. We eat in silence, while Mohun feeds him soup in his room. Dada does not want to join us at the table any longer.

He falls asleep on the swing while speaking in disjointed sentences.

Then, listening to the radio, he turns to me and whispers, 'Next year in Jerusalem...go, go.' I do not answer. 'If I had taken my daughters to Israel, they would have been happy,' he tells me. Then he slides into a monologue in Marathi, complimenting Leah on the colour of her sari.

Julie and Sinora have been calling Mother at the office to ask if they are needed. But Mother says she can manage. I think he wants to see his daughters, but knows that they will not come to see him. They have chosen to believe that he is not seriously ill and have promised Mother that they will come and see their father as soon as they have the time. Mother says wearily, 'He has no time left.' I hear Mohun crying and telling Mother, 'He is going.'

Everybody is trying to protect me from the truth. I know he is dying and I feel a strange stillness. I see Mother crying.

She is changing from hard stone to soft water and although she finds it difficult to express her love for her father, she dreads the thought of losing him. She has also begun to feel a certain affection for Mohun, probably because he loves Danieldada. They help each other cook, and talk about him, and she feels she now knows her father better through Mohun. Through him she finds out that Dada loves the memory of her mother and needs to free himself from the guilt of her death, and feels a stirring of love for him.

I now know that everything has an end. Nothing lasts. The walls around the city fall into the dry river bed. Weakening fortresses, open doors, watch towers without eyes, empty nests. Mani hopes Dada's end will come without much suffering. 'We suffer a bad end because of the sins of our last life,' she says.

Perhaps Danieldada will have a painful end in his next birth because he has given pain to Leah in this birth. Mother says, 'Our god punishes those who break a commandment.'

They cover his eyes with earth from Jerusalem. I take some in my fingers and sprinkle it over his eyes. Brown, dry earth of the Promised Land, textured exactly like that of my surrogate motherland.

Yards of white cloth, stitched on the sewing machine by Mother, Granny and Aunty Hannah. His shroud. The pantaloons, the long coat, the cummerbund and the cap...they put white socks on his feet and tie a sprig of fragrant leaves to his hands with a handkerchief. He is now ready for his last journey.

Hands dusty with the earth of both lands, and wet with my tears, I wonder about Jerusalem. Samuel stands still like a statue over the grave, the wax from the candle burning his hands.

I want to ask him from where we come and where we go. We do not know from where. But we know why. From sure death. Expulsion. Exile. Homes broken, disrupted, burnt, from ruin to ruin with the hidden Book. The Book lost in the shipwreck. Eyes watching King Solomon's golden temple. The Exodus. Crossing the sea. The ten lost tribes calling out to one another in lonely, faraway lands.

A long journey into the dark night, following the silk route from Yemen. Rome? Spain? Navgaon. Pressing oil from coconuts under the sleepy eyes of the ox. Before Christ? After Christ? The story of exile, the Book lost in the Arabian Sea. Closing in on the freedom of our minds, our breath, our thoughts, our prayer to the god without a face in the land of eyes.

Jerusalem, with the golden stones. Eyes swimming like fishes in the turquoise Sea of Galilee. The story repeats itself. Farewell. Leave everything and start all over again. Circumcise your sons. Observe the Shabbat.

Skins mingling, mixing, changing colour.

Graves on the shores of Navgaon. Six couples crouching together in the womb of the earth. Mysterious dwelling places of my ancestors. I am just the seed of a buried tree. 'Dig the graves and we will know who we are.' High on rum, Uncle Menachem bangs his fist on the table. Granny is shocked by such blasphemy and we cower in fear.

I want to hide in Pratibha's temple and offer lotuses to her god just like the gopis. Krishna, hide me under your mantle. I could be safe under the Mount Govardhan that he holds so easily on his little finger. Come what may, rain, storm or lightning, I can huddle there with his cows.

Granny says, 'Say the Shema to drive away the bhoots in your mind. Kiss the mezuzah when you enter the house. With the mark on the door, the bad spirits cannot enter.' I do not have the courage to tell her that the scroll does not help.

I need something more real. Perhaps Granny would understand, because she refers to our god as deva and the synagogue as deval, so her god must have some sort of face like Hanuman or Kali. But she does not use the word prarthana for prayers, she refers to it as namaaz. Perhaps she would not understand, because I know she is annoyed with Uncle Gerard's devotion to Saibaba.

The squirrels are waiting to be fed by Danieldada. The empty swing creaks. The parrot and the peacock are silent.

aunty jerusha

T he unoccupied swing in
the open verandah scares
me and the mezuzah
cannot drive away the visions I have
of Danieldada. I need respite from
the house in Shahibagh and return
to Dilhi Darwaza.

They say that Danieldada's spirit
will linger for forty days and Mother

thinks it would be better for me to sleep with Granny in the other house.

But Granny has changed, she worries all the time. Aunty Jerusha is returning from England. She is a doctor, and Granny's eldest daughter. The house has changed a lot since she left and Granny worries that she may be put off by the mess. I am afraid to meet her. We the ordinary mortals who plough through our daily chores, are in awe of our fascinating aunt.

The whole household welcomes her at the railway station with marigold garlands. Standing in the doorway, fair and slender, in shoes with square heels, narrow black skirt, beige silk shirt, a string of pearls, a bright pink scarf and a neat French roll, she looks just like a picture from one of the English magazines Aunty Hannah reads. Our eyes cannot believe that this beautiful woman belongs to us. How will I ever lick the chutney off my fingers in her presence ? But I do, and she joins in and keeps me company.

It is difficult to accept her presence in the house, even if she puts everybody at ease, behaving as though she had never left. But she ignores the curious looks at her legs and turns a deaf ear to Granny's request that she wear a sari. She ends the conversation with the simple answer, 'I cannot walk in a sari.'

She sleeps in the same room as Granny, Malkha and Samuel.

I return to Shahibagh with a promise from my cousins that they will tell me all about Aunty Jerusha's nightclothes. Much to everybody's shock, she wears what she calls a kimono, and Aunty Hannah is horrified, 'What will the servants say?'

Aunty Hannah and Mother sleep in their saris.

This spells the beginning of trouble and Samuel says there are endless arguments. As for him, he feels extremely honoured to be in the same room with someone so smart. This again seems to bother Aunty, and she insists that she needs a room to herself. It is obvious that the three women do not agree on anything and Uncle maintains an uneasy silence. He cannot take sides.

She takes interest in our homework and spends time with me in Shahibagh. She upsets Mother by suggesting that I should be allowed to wear smart, well-fitting clothes and learn to dance. Mother cuts her short, 'In our family we don't.' She tries to argue with Mother and even cries, saying that she had never been allowed to do anything she wanted. She has bitter memories of her own father. Punishment, and hard work at school and college. No games, no laughter. I think she must be stronger than Mother.

Sometimes I think she must hate everybody.

Father says that she was brought up to be the breadwinner of the family because his father had no faith in the boys. Offers from suitors were rejected without consulting her and she had grown convinced that she was ugly and did not possess the qualities that would make a good wife. She had given herself up to the service of the family and humanity.

And so she has returned, stamping out all thought of romance, refusing a proposal of marriage from a colleague who had recently lost his wife.

Granny says, 'It was impossible to find an educated match for Jerusha. Perhaps a Baghdadi Jew would have been good enough for her, but they consider us uncultured and very Indian in our habits, rather desi. And in such a house there is no guarantee that a girl will be treated well, so she is safer in her own mother's house.' Unknowingly, Granny closes Raphael's doors on my face. I have no right to dream of a person who considers me to be of a low caste.

It is difficult to take life in one's stride as Aunty Jerusha does. She listens to music, sees a Hindi film once a week with the family, and manages to keep her face expressionless during the love scenes.

Once in a while she makes bread pudding or strawberry jelly and custard for the whole family.

I am a little jealous of her. Ever since her arrival, Granny is less attentive to me, and concentrates only on her. Father says she feels guilty, because even when their father was unduly strict with his daughter, Granny never intervened. Nor did she ask her husband to give Aunty Jerusha a chance to decide whether she wanted to accept a proposal or not.

Aunty does not care for anything except her work at the general hospital. She is at ease with herself and I admire and envy her at the same time. Once a year she arranges a tour of India for a Parsi or Anglo- Indian group, with special shopping trips to Bombay.

Uncle and Father say that Aunty Jerusha should be an example to us. She has brought books on Judaism from London and reads out passages, 'The lord is my shepherd, I shall not want...' Despite her fancy clothes, I think Aunty is a very spiritual person. I now realize that God means service to humanity.

Deeply influenced by Aunty Jerusha, Malkha has started preparing herself for the future. She says there is no point in dreaming about Joel and she is too scared to look beyond him. Boys from other communities scare her. They are too different and make her feel uncomfortable. She is no longer interested in becoming a film star, so when the family goes to the cinema, she reads while Amina watches over her.

Nothing lasts forever. Aunty has been offered the post of director at a hospital in Surendranagar. She needs a place of her own. It is understood that Granny will go with her. The possessions are divided between Father, Uncle and Granny, more between the women than the men. Aunty Hannah with her aggressive arguments gets a larger share, Mother gets the least. In a temper, Granny throws at Aunty Hannah the keys to the steel cupboards and the storerooms. The house now belongs to her.

the house of mangos

I had always waited for the summer with a sense of pleasure. The house in Dilhi Darwaza would be filled with the fragrance of ripe Alphonso mangos spread out on straw mats. Our lives revolved around mangos: pickled, raw, dried, ripe and over ripe.

It was then that uncles, aunts and cousins of all sizes filled the house and there were endless discussions on lineage, who was related to whom, how and in what way; the question of whether the Jews had come to India during the Spanish Inquisition or after the fall of Solomon's second Temple; and had there really been a shipwreck or had we used the silk route.

Half asleep we would listen to these stories and wonder which family we would eventually belong to, staring at the men with white beards and big moustaches, and the women, overweight and matronly. We'd exchange shy looks with some cousin or the other who may have been dreaming about us, as Malkha and Joel had done.

But, because of my loyalty to Samuel and the Baghdadi Krishna, I refused to look at any of my cousins and lost out on the family matchmaking by treating them all as brothers. Anyway, I found them so narrow in their interests and hobbies that I would not have survived being in love for more than ten minutes. Except perhaps with Emmanuel who had returned from London with a stack of waltz records. He did give me long exploring looks which flattered me although I was then still in school. When he offered to teach me to waltz, Malkha, closer to him in age, had turned more than green with jealousy. She still holds it against me.

The family had been shocked, but had laughed falsely, not wanting to look like small-town folks, and Father, stern-faced, had wound the record player with the huge polished brass horn while I stood with my hand cold and stiff in Emmanuel's. My face was flushed and my heart beat fast. When he started dancing, holding me tight in his arms, breathing rum in my hair, I could barely move, yet I could hear him whispering in my ear, 'Perhaps we could get married, you are beautiful.' He let me go suddenly saying, 'Ah, she dances like a horse. She will never learn.'

The council of elders laughed in relief, but Mother stared at me as though she would have liked to spank me.

When she found me alone she whispered, 'You should have taken my permission.'

But she did look at me with new eyes when Emmanuel's family asked Father whether we would consider an alliance between our families. The answer was, 'No, she is too young, she has still to make a career for herself.'

Fine curly hair had only just begun to appear between my legs, and Mother had stitched me a vest that restricted my breathing. Helping me into it, she told me that it was strange that anybody should want to marry me, because I was quite ordinary.

Samuel felt betrayed at my dancing with Emmanuel and Malkha was hurt too. So when Emmanuel's father later asked for Malkha's hand for his son, she refused him because she was his second choice, and anyway she was in love with Joel.

Years later when Malkha did come closer to her dream, she refused to marry Joel because from his letters she felt he was not the man she was looking for. He was rather dull and not interested in all that Malkha liked, and the prospect of cooking curries for him in a land far away from home horrified her. Besides, the Gerard family wanted an assurance that Malkha would not work outside the house. The wording of the letter was such that Malkha got angry and told Uncle Menachem to inform the Gerards that they had no business to force decisions on her. She refused to be their bonded labourer for life, though Aunty Hannah saw nothing wrong in her staying at home as long as she had a Jewish husband. But for once the council of elders was split, as some of them favoured careers more than weddings.

Malkha was further disillusioned with Joel when he later married our distant cousin Rebecca. Uncle Menachem philosophically commented, 'And, so the tribe must increase.'

the crack in the wall

Mani tells me a story. Late one night a stranger knocks on the doors of a city. When the doors are opened, he says that he has something important to say...he has dreamt of a swarm of locusts over the city.

There is no evidence to prove that he belongs to the city and the city fathers are suspicious. How can someone who does not belong to the city dream about it? So he is put in prison and is warned that he could be hanged. Nevertheless, the grains are stored carefully. When the locusts do arrive the food is safe and the man is given a reward. Later he discloses that his mother was a daughter of the city. From then on the doors are no longer locked, because the man explains that one cannot see far enough unless the doors are kept open.

I like this story. It has a sense of mystery. Who was this man? It is obvious he was not known to the people of the city. Did he care so much for them that he felt he had to help them even at the cost of his own life? Unknown danger fascinates me. Did the man lie about his mother? Did he play upon the sentiments of the people and open the city to the greater danger of an invasion? Was the man a spy?

I think Ahmedabad is like the city in this story, always throbbing with a sense of danger. After a spell of heavy rains, the last of the fortress walls near the Sabarmati develops a deep crack. People are being evacuated. It has been decided that a part of the walls should be demolished. We read about the controversy in the Gujarati papers. Historians protest. But the safety of the people is more important. I cannot imagine Ahmedabad without this last remnant of its past glory.

Women from the Shahpur slum carry away bricks and stones to reinforce their shacks of tin and thatch held together with clay. The wound in the wall grows larger every day and becomes a thoroughfare for cows, dogs and beggars who wash themselves in the raging Sabarmati, red with the blood of her people. Swords are drawn. The creepers and flowers in the stone carving are dying. The walled city is under curfew. There are guns and rifles. Outsiders, say the newspapers, are creating disturbances. Now the gates cannot be closed. Who was that man who opened the gates? Was he right or wrong? But windows are closed. Doors locked. What is your religion? Who are you? From where do you come? We are burning in the fires of hell.

Father's and Anwar's pigeons are dead. Father had always considered the birds 'theirs' even after he had moved to Shahibagh. He visited Anwar every Saturday afternoon.

Broken wooden drawers. Blood and feathers. Anwar lies on a charpoy with his hand fractured. Perhaps he will never be able to work again. Uncle Menachem says, 'We lost only the victoria. It was burnt and the horses are in a state of shock. Perhaps we can sell them to the Jain temple. They have been looking for white horses for their ceremonial chariot.' He has decided to sell the house and move to a cosmopolitan housing colony. Possibly with Parsis and Christians as neighbours. The house is sold to Rahimbhai Hadvaid, the bone-setter.

Mani says the riot is like a rakshasa. One does not know how to destroy him. It is impossible to locate the demon's heart. He hides it in dungeons, in caged parrots or in the middle of his brows. His heart is a riddle, the answer to which is known only to the demon himself. And so he lives on, indestructible and dangerous.

Without the house we are like orphans. The house at Dilhi Darwaza was like a mother's lap, soft and comforting. Now I know how Mother feels.

The heart of our house, the dining table, is sold. It was too big and cumbersome and there was no door large enough for it to pass through. We lost another grandparent in the table. And the sense of togetherness along with the charred victoria.

Mother and Aunty Hannah vie with each other in buying green and blue formica-topped tables, gas stoves and cookers. The warm glow of brass and copper has been replaced by hard steel. Father cannot impose upon Mother the choice of another table. It is her territory. Danieldada's simple teakwood table was sold in the river bed bazaar, and Mother protects the new one against scratches and stains. Memories are fading and the distances between houses extend into hearts.

laxmi

Father is doing well and everyone says I am Laxmi, the goddess of prosperity whose presence brings abundance. I am flattered. I see myself standing on a lotus, showering gold coins on the world. I am wearing a red saree with a gold border and a jewelled crown.

During Divali, I help Pratibha arrange the earthen lamps on her terrace. The sparklers and crackers make her house look like swarg and we, the apsaras in our ghaghras, draw multicoloured rangolis at the entrance to the house. Pratibha says, 'If the rangoli is beautiful and the lamps are still burning, Laxmi enters the house at midnight.' I must ask Uncle Menachem whether Laxmi is similar to the prophet Elijah. We used to open the door and wait for him during the feast of Passover in Granny's house. My house is dark as I crawl into bed. I would like to light a lamp, and draw a lotus on our doorstep. But I know I must never draw a swastika.

I, the virgin of the house, am the auspicious Laxmi. Father's furniture is in great demand. One of the pujaris from the Kali temple has great faith in the quality of his work and says it is all because of Bhadra Kali that Father is doing well. Ever since he made some carved stools for the temple and presented a divan to the pujari, the goddess favours us. The pujari comes to visit us in a white dhoti, a red shawl thrown over his shoulders, a big red dot on his forehead and a small tuft dangling from his shaven head.

Like Subhadra, he never sits in the drawing room and does not eat or drink anything that we offer him. Father has told Mother not to serve him tea or coffee, because it would be embarrassing if he refused. He questions Father about our eating habits and Father tries to set his mind at ease by telling him about our dietary laws, but he is not convinced. Our neighbours do not seem to mind the egg shells and bones that stray dogs and crows ferret out of the garbage and scatter around their houses. At Dilhi Darwaza, Subhadra's family often used to complain and quarrel with us about this. Now they too are planning to sell their house and move to a safer area. A petrol bomb was thrown into their courtyard the other night. They want to rent a house on the other side of the river. Father says that people with the same eating habits normally group together. 'But I am different,' he says, 'I am a Gujarati.' Aunty Hannah could never tolerate comments on her food habits, so Uncle has bought a house in a co-operative society where their neighbours are meat eaters; not that he cares who eats what. Discussions like these make me feel like a cannibal.

Hasmukh Mistry tells me a story about the pujari. The goddess had appeared to his grandfather in a dream. She was buried under the fort, she'd said, and asked him to unearth her. He rejoiced when he found her. Shining black stone with living eyes that answered the prayers of the faithful and punished the sinners. It seems that their gods need to breathe. I still have problems with my god being mere breath.

Mistry is a simple soul, ignorant of Mother's views on idols and godmen, and has brought upon our house a great dharm sankat, a religious crisis. His footpath days are over and he has bought a small house in the suburbs of Chandlodia, near the lake. He now lives there with his wife and children. He had made a vow to offer eleven coconuts and a box of fifty-one pedas to Bhadra Kali in the presence of his family and ours.

Mother refuses to go with him to the temple but Father does not mind. He has been to many mosques and temples and nothing touches him. He does not revel in them like Danieldada, but does not reject them either. For him, Mistry is important and nothing can stop him from going to the Bhadra Kali temple.

When Mistry realizes that Mother will not go with him, he sits on the floor holding his head. If he does not fulfil his promise to Kali she will destroy all that he's achieved. Father looks at Mother accusingly and I can see that they are afraid. Both Mother and Father. Nothing must fall apart in their little world because of an ungranted wish. Mother agrees to go, but on condition that she need not bow her head to another god.

I am excited when I step into the temple. Drumbeats, brass bells, a cloud of sindoor. Kali, dark as the night, is dressed in a brocade sari; eyes like Subhadra's look into mine. The pujari is pleased to see Father. He breaks the coconuts and returns the prasad after the aarti with some special laddus for us. Quickly I follow Mistry and his wife, and touch the flame the way Granny blesses the Shabbat candle. Mother's eyes watch me as I stand there, head bent and palms joined together in supplication. There is a sudden rush of people and we have to move away. On the way out, I ring the brass bell. Mother does not speak to me for two full days and then asks me, 'Why did you do it, why?' I have only one answer, 'I like the sound of the bells. Why don't we have some drums and gongs at the synagogue?' She tries to explain the shofar, but her answers do not satisfy me. 'If you question everything, you will suffer,' her eyes plead with me.

mumtaz begum

S he has two names, Mani
and Mumtaz. Like my
great uncle, Shamaji
Samuel Dandekar, our family hero,
the one who took part in the freedom
struggle and makes us feel ashamed
of all our other ancestors who were
loyal to the British. Mumtaz alias
Mani was given two names by her

father Rasoolbhai, royal perfumer to the Nawab of Palanpur. After his wife had lost four children, the fifth was delivered alive by a Hindu midwife named Mani, who had accepted Rasoolbhai as her brother, 'mooh bola bhai', literally meaning, 'he is my brother because I say so'. The overjoyed father had wanted to give her gifts but she had instead asked that the child be named after her. She had died soon after the baby was born and Rasoolbhai had considered this to be an omen. It was the midwife's last wish to live through the newborn baby, who would one day learn to deliver babies herself.

This is Mani's version which I believe. But Uncle Menachem says that it used to be the custom to give children two names to camouflage their identity during times of communal tension.

Mani does not ever call herself Mumtaz, and her face does not betray her background. One sees in her eyes the memory of terrible loss, emptiness and homelessness. And yet, it would not have always been so. She had learnt from her father the art of making perfumes from flowers. But now there is no reason for her to make perfumes or wear them. Tobacco is the only flavour she knows. It deadens all pain.

She is not happy, and feels isolated from her kind who live together in groups between Dilhi Darwaza and Kalupur Darwaza. In Shahibagh she is alone despite having Mohun, Mistry and us for company and feels troubled when Pratibha's widowed aunts question her about her background. She is touched that the men of our house accept the food and water she offers them but is afraid that if something were to happen, she would be killed, burnt alive, or raped.

This is not the Mani I knew. She no longer spins wonderful
tales but instead sits brooding for hours, like the Dariapur beggar.
She reminds me of the old horses that pull the remaining
ghodagadis at Delhi Chakla, flies milling around their eyes and
heads drooping as they whisk their tails to the sounds of the
autorickshaws we now prefer.

She asks Mother for a day off to visit her friends at Dilhi
Darwaza. She's never done that before except the day when she
borrowed Granny's umbrella to go and see the unusual sight of
the floods. She had said, 'When our river floods, she races like
a hundred galloping horses. It is rare to see her touching the
base of the bridge.' She called the iron structure as the lakadiya
pul, the wooden bridge of her grandfather's days. The passionate
river excites Mani, 'On most days the river is like a desert.' I
wonder if Mani is talking about herself.

Lately Mother has been impatient with Mani and suspects
that she is looking for work elsewhere. But she does allow her a
day off and Mani surprises everybody by having a bath under
the garden tap, an old sari wrapped around her. She lets me
watch while she puts on a freshly washed sari and also permits
me to look into her tin box. It has a broken mirror, two saris, a
torn petticoat, a multicoloured poster of the Kaaba, and a small
wooden perfume box lined with velvet, holding a little bottle of
jasmine attar, the only remaining keepsake to remind her of her
family. She opens it, allows me to swim in the fragrance for a
moment, and then closes it again. She never uses it because she
is a widow. Then she gives me her blessings by touching her
closed fists to her temples, 'When you get married, baby, I will
bathe you with this attar,' she says.

One day, after witnessing a stabbing on the street, Mani does not return to us. Days of police interrogations and court cases follow. The heroine of Dilhi Darwaza stays with Amina's family and Hannahbai's allegations are forgotten. She has decided to wed Hasanchacha, a widower who is a peon at the court. Over endless cups of bitter-sweet tea on the footpath opposite Ahmedshah's mosque, she has agreed to be his begum.

Mani, now Mumtaz Begum, arrives in an autorickshaw to tell us about her engagement, bringing tiffin carriers full of warm biryani. She is no longer homeless, but has abandoned me, her adopted daughter, leaving behind only the essence of her spirit. She has gifted me the perfume box.

the prophet

Uncle Menachem is waiting for the prophet Elijah.

Aunty is in hospital, where she has delivered a baby brother for Samuel. Malkha is embarrassed and Samuel spends all his time with the Syed family boys at Dilhi Darwaza. Uncle has built himself a tent of

thick khadi in the middle of the drawing room and he fasts for
forty days, eating a little at sundown. He will not see the face of
the child unless the prophet appears before him.

To believe, he must see.

Aunty is in tears and everybody depends on Mother. Early in
the morning before leaving for work, she goes to the hospital
with some food for Aunty Hannah. Aunty is grateful, and cries
every time she sees Mother, and praises her 'large heart'. Mother
shrugs it off as duty.

Granny rushes to Ahmedabad and stays for a couple of
days—she cannot leave Jerusha alone with the servants for
longer than that. She sympathises with Aunty Hannah about
Uncle's madness and tells her the story of his birth. Her husband,
our grandfather Isaji, had been so taken with Mahatma Gandhi,
that she had suffered in the same way as Aunty Hannah. Gandhi's
ashram on the banks of the Sabarmati had become an obsession
with him because of his hero Shamaji Uncle. He took to spinning
and wearing khadi, abstained from meat, ate the simple ashram
food and drank goat's milk. When Granny was in the eighth
month of her pregnancy, he had gone away to the ashram saying
he should not be contacted. So he had not known about the
birth of the child—perhaps he had not wanted to know—and
Granny had thought she had lost him forever.

Like Aunty Hannah, she had cried for days. When Uncle was
three months old, Grandfather had suddenly appeared at the
front door, and Granny had been afraid that he would ask her
for alms, and then disappear again. Instead he had sat down on
the floor in padmasan and looked at the child. He had then

sung the ashram bhajan and Granny had cried and laughed at the same time and accused him of not understanding her pain. He had responded by covering her shoulders with a white khadi sari he had spun himself and they had wept in each other's arms.

'Our men are all a little eccentric, but one should not worry. After a while they become normal,' she says. Isaji had finally given in to family pressure and stayed home but had continued to work for Bapu, disappearing at times and then resurfacing again. He disapproved of anyone in the family working for the British and that, says Granny, is another reason why the family has always been uncomfortable with my mother's father.

During Uncle's spells of eccentricity everybody turns to Father. Everyone is afraid that madness, the genetic disease that Uncle dreads, might have struck.

The small house is in a mess, with things from Dilhi Darwaza crammed everywhere. The prophet does not appear and Uncle is disappointed and embarrassed. He tries to bring back normalcy but Aunty has vowed that she will never forgive him. He is depressed and it is difficult not to sympathise with him. The event has made him lose faith and he feels cheated. With hair falling over his forehead and a glass of rum in his hand, he says dramatically, 'My god has failed me.'

I am sure any moment now lightning will strike our house and Aunty Hannah, ever curious, will become a pillar of salt.

Nothing happens.

Over glasses which seem to empty quickly, Father agrees readily with Uncle's values and philosophy and we look on in silence.

Without Granny we feel lost at the synagogue. In fact nobody takes us there any more. Even if we did go there, we would not know what to do. We do not know if we are gaining or losing something.

I stop myself from asking Uncle why my new cousin is being circumcised. I think I know what his answer will be. 'Because it is hygienic. If we were following rituals we would have had a bar mitzvah for Samuel.'

Like the greasy, unused menorah and the dusty mezuzah on the door, which we rarely remember to kiss, I suppose some things will remain a mystery. We have different lives, each family in a different corner, meeting once a month for dinner in one of the houses. Most of our relatives, including our Bombay cousins, have left for Israel. We receive wedding invitations, announcements of births, deaths and engagements, New Year cards and Hanukkah wishes. Photographs of cousins in dresses, shorts, jeans, short hair and army uniform.

All we remember are the weddings which made us cry, bhel puri at Chowpatty, pomfret fish and Aunty Shoshonah sitting on a low stool and slitting the necks of chicken in accordance with the kosher laws. Our relatives used to buy goat's meat only on Fridays from the synagogue and we used to feel like heathens as we continued to buy ours from the butcher at Dilhi Darwaza. We used to shock Aunty Shoshonah with confused questions about why we could not eat fish without scales and chapatis with ghee.

Weddings make us cry, because, somewhere deep inside us we know that we can never attain the beauty which our parents had experienced. They now dictate our values and philosophy, and so we have to remain untouched and cannot look back lest we become pillars of salt. The song of the groom calling to the bride, the white veil held with silk roses, bridesmaids in short white dresses and tiaras, the white purity of the sari, gloves and high-heeled shoes, gold bangles, necklaces and earrings, the exchanging of rings and the sips of wine, the anxiety—'Will the groom succeed in breaking the glass with his foot?'—, the blessings, the food, the meeting of eyes, the dreams of young virgins at the mehendi ceremony, the bride, wearing a green sari and green bangles, symbolic of freshness and fertility, returning to her mother's house with the groom, to discover her womanhood. These are not for us.

It was all very different at Pratibha's cousin's wedding where the bride and the groom circled the fire, the pallav of her red brocade sari tied to the groom's shawl, their hands clasped together under the cloth.

The eternal couple.

After the ceremonies, the bride leaves in a sea of tears and once she reaches her husband's house, where the five virgins wait to welcome her, it must remain her home for ever.

We are the virgins—Pratibha, Vatsala, Mandakini, Ketaki and I.

An old aunt objects, 'But that one is not one of us.' I feel cold and alone, but then someone answers reassuringly, 'No, she is just like us.' It makes me want to disown my name, a name which exposes me. I am what they are not.

And what am I ?

Human, says Father.

Although we look alike, Pratibha cannot help asking me, like Subhadra before her, 'If you are not a Christian, a Parsi or a Muslim, what are you?'

'We are different,' says Uncle Menachem. 'You are too young to understand, but there are subtle differences.'

I miss Granny. She leads an uneventful life with Aunty who writes to us once a month. Granny sends us her blessings and scribbles her name in a childish scrawl in Marathi below her thumb impression. Aunty Jerusha is teaching her to read and write.

vishwakarma

As for us, each morning is no different from any other. They all revolve around Father's workshop and Mother's daily routine.

Mohun finds it difficult to cope with Mother's timetable and respectfully informs her of his decision to leave. Danieldada was his family. He has no other and does not feel a sense of belonging with my mother. If Danieldada is watching from up there, it would please him to see that his portrait has now found a place among Mohun's gods. Every morning it is garlanded with a string of marigold or jasmine flowers which he threads himself. He also spends some of Mother's precious morning hours praying to her father and makes her feel guilty of not doing enough to preserve his memory.

Mohun has decided to buy a roadside dhaba on the Bombay highway, where he will sell chicken curry and kebabs. It will be named 'Danbaba ka dhabha' after Danieldada. He has saved money while working for us and now wants to try something new. The roadside restaurant will have a big photograph of his patron saint, complete with sandalwood garlands and agarbattis. Mother is not amused at the idea of her Jewish father as a folk god. Moreover, she thinks it mocks the memory of her mother.

In the secrecy of the kitchen, when Mother is not there, I listen to Mohun's plans and help him select his best recipes. I know I will never see his dhabha unless someday Father takes me there, but I promise to visit him when I am 'big'. He is touched and says, 'Baby, you have a good head and a great heart just like your Danieldada.'

Mother doesn't like it when Mistry refers to her husband as his Vishwakarma, the god of artisans. The business is doing well and soon they will shift their workshop to an industrial shed in Asarwa. I ask endless questions and Mother says I remind her of her father. 'You must be quiet if you wish to find answers.'

Pratibha feels that I would have less trouble with Mother if I accepted things as they are. She herself dare not ask her parents so many questions. But then there is a difference between us— she need never ask questions anyway, as everything is clear to her: her religion, her history, her caste and the code of behaviour she is expected to follow.

Slowly I find there is a strange silence creeping upon the council of elders. The Bibles gather dust and no candles are lit on Shabbat. They have no answers to our questions and we embarrass them by mirroring their ignorance.

Granny had brought us up encouraging us to believe that when we did not understand something about our religion, we should ask questions. As children, Samuel and I had nicknamed the grown-ups of our family the council of elders and long back on a Passover in the old house, I the youngest child, remember asking all sorts of questions.

Now the packets of matza bread are never opened and Mother has forgotten how to spread the table in memory of the crossing of the sea. And I ask myself, are you the evil child who forgets Passover? I am the princess imprisoned in the citadel and there is no escape. I am my own prisoner and feel as if everyone has deserted me.

I see my parents early in the morning and late at night and wish Mother were like Aunty Hannah. I want her to cook with Amina, read women's magazines, plan trips to the cinema, and take long afternoon naps.

I'd like Mother to become pregnant so that she'd be compelled to stay at home. It would be fun to have a brother or a sister for company. Now there is only Rukmanibai, our new cook, who seems to be dumb. She cannot speak because of the tobacco stuffed in her left cheek. I feel hurt when Mother says Rukmanibai is far more competent than either Mani or Mohun.

It seems unlikely that Mother will give me a sister. Mother and Father sleep in different beds and I still sleep in the same room with them. I asked for a room of my own when Danieldada died, but Mother said it was not necessary. Mani used to say that Mother is like a holy goddess devoted to Father, that she is spiritual. I do not understand. If Mother is holy then Father also must be so. I never saw anything happen between them, at least, not the things Subhadra used to see happening between her parents. The extra rooms are being used as Father's storerooms and library.

Bored in school, lonely at home, and hopelessly in love with Raphael, I write poems about mirages. The Hindi film is my saviour and I cry with the tortured heroines on Radio Ceylon. Raphael's mother scares me with her red lipstick, chiffon saris, Queen Elizabeth hairstyle, high heels and the large handbag shaped like a boat. She is a physicist and her son is also considered brilliant.

I could never be a part of that family.

Samuel is no longer possessive about me. He reads my poetry and looks doubtful. 'Do you like Elvis?' he asks. I feel frozen for I am addicted to Hindi film songs. Samuel thinks I am hopeless. He at least makes an effort. 'True,' he says, 'it is tough in our family with the ghazals, Begum Akhtar, the Dagar brothers, and Saigal, but one must try to rise above all that, like me and my violin. If you want to kindle Raphi's interest, you must develop yourself. Try to understand his way of life. I had lunch with his family last week. They are a little anglicised, like your Danieldada. That's all.' 'Then,' I tell him, 'there is no problem.'

He looks at me strangely and continues, 'I think you could be more comfortable with someone like me...no?'

I do not know whether he is proposing. I almost ask him if he means what he says, because that would make things simpler. But we are only fifteen and Mother is of the opinion that I am still a child. Yet, most of our aunts and uncles were married at fifteen.

A damri rises and clouds of dust move in circles stirring up the dry leaves. Samuel crosses over to shut the window as the dust blows into our eyes and the subject is closed. I feel like the dry leaves, sometimes reaching the sky, then falling back into the dust.

prince of baghdad

We now have a car and a telephone. Mistry had advised Father to buy the car before Dussera and when it arrived he garlanded the bonnet with a string of yellow marigolds and performed a little pooja with a clay lamp in a steel thali, applied sindoor on it, and only then allowed Father to use it.

It is now easier to go to the cinema and meet Samuel and Malkha, although it is boring to speak to Malkha. She has accepted her fate and is no longer interested in anything but her studies. She has no questions and if she has any problems, we do not know about them. But Samuel and I have long conversations and Aunty Hannah is afraid we will fall in love, the way she fell in love with Uncle. As for Mother, she believes that Samuel is my brother and there could never be anything more between us.

On the phone, Samuel tells me that Raphael is being sent to London for higher studies as his father feels that there is no future for him here. I listen silently.

He asks, 'Are you there?'

I mumble something and knowing that he cannot see my face, I gather enough courage to ask him, 'Does he...'

'What?'

'...love?'

'Yes.'

'How do you know?'

'He told me.'

'Why didn't you tell me?'

'I forgot.'

I whisper, 'When?'

'Last week.'

'What did he say?'

'About what?'

I whisper again, 'Me.'

'Oh! He said my cousin is very beautiful.'

'Me?' I ask, looking down at the chipped nail of my toe.

He says, 'Yes.'

I ask him, 'Now what?'

'He wants to see you,' he says.

'You know that's impossible, Mother would kill me.'

'He says he wants to come and look at Uncle's wood carvings. You know, to buy a few gifts to take with him now that he is going abroad.'

'Will you come with him?'

'No. Aunty would smell a rat.'

I am already dreaming of the future and he cuts in, 'You can at least thank me.'

I apologise and say, 'But Samuel, it is useless, he is going away.'

'True,' he agrees, 'but he might propose before he leaves.'

And then he hangs up with a bit of brotherly advice, 'Don't let him know you have not even heard of Elvis.'

That evening Raphael calls on us. Mother keeps me indoors and I watch him from behind the curtains with my heart beating faster and faster. Like Krishna he has his flute with him, and had we been left alone he would surely have played it for me. Our eyes meet, but Mother calls me from the kitchen and asks me to keep an eye on the tea while she prepares the tray. I offer to serve tea, but she shakes her head and says, 'It's all right, I'll do it myself. You always spill everything,' and then turns around and tells me, 'mind the curry.'

I can hear him, talking like an adult. Why does he not ask for me and say, 'Uncle, I've come to meet your daughter.'

The curtain separates us. It is like a Hindu marriage, I tell myself, with the antarpat between us. It is the moment before the meeting of the eyes. I switch off the stove and pretend to read by the lily pond.

As he leaves, he smiles at me and I watch him like Echo pining for Narcissus.

Samuel is a liar.

I refuse to speak to him on the phone. He wants to know whether anything has happened but I tell Mother to say, 'She is not here,' whenever he calls, and late that night he rushes to our house on his bicycle. I am brushing my teeth. Mother is surprised, but he does not say anything to her. He pulls my plait and demands angrily with bloodshot eyes, 'Why don't you want to speak to me?' Even before I can answer, the phone rings and I hear Mother pacifying an anxious Aunty Hannah. It is decided that Samuel will spend the night in our house and return home in the morning. When Aunty asks for Samuel he refuses to speak to her and tells Mother, 'I am a grown-up boy and I can do whatever I want.' Without letting go of my plait, he scolds me, 'You dream too much. Do you know some people consider us to have black blood. Understand?'

Father, more patient and conversant with the ways of the men of our family, sits him down at the dining table and offers him a glass of beer. Mother immediately accuses Father of spoiling the boy, but he says sharply, 'He had a sip of brandy when he was circumcised, so it is okay.'

And then Samuel flares up and declares that he is not interested in any of that Jewish stuff. No one has ever seen him like that. Father tries to explain something about King David and Solomon and their many wives and their progeny. 'Blood never becomes black,' says Father, 'it becomes increasingly richer.'

That night I sleep in my mother's bed, her legs entwined with mine, and Samuel sleeps in mine. The monsoon clouds gather over the horizon and in the morning I hear the distant call of the koel. Outside the window, the mango trees are in bloom.

next year in jerusalem

scape is impossible. I
dream of Vishnu's last
avatar, Kalki, the
destroyer of evil, who will come
riding a horse. 'Like the Messiah,'
says Granny, 'and the doors will
open in Yerushalem.' Granny always
pronounces Jerusalem with a 'Y'.
Her hands play with my bare wrists.
'Where,' she asks, 'are the bangles?
You must wear bangles.'

Aunty Jerusha has returned to Ahmedabad to practise medicine. She has bought a flat on the other side of the river in Ambavadi, near Uncle's house. Yet none of us meet as we used to earlier. They rarely go to the synagogue, but never forget to light the Shabbat candles. In our house not even that is done.

Mother allows me to spend Navaratri with Pratibha and Vatsala. Under a full moon, we sing and dance, small perforated pots on our heads, symbolic of the sky and the womb, offerings to the mother goddess Durga. The Dandiya-raas and Garba dance give me greater pleasure than anything else.

In all this, Granny—her face, a little older and more wrinkled than before—sitting in her hall of faded photographs, remains the only memory of our history and past. I realize that she has grown older when our Israeli relatives come to visit us.

Uncles and aunts, like spreading creepers. Oversized matrons with heavy double chins from the land of milk and honey, protruding stomachs stuffed into jeans and skirts or nylon saris with large geranium flowers, high heels, uncared for hair, sometimes tied in a ponytail or rolled into an untidy bun. They wear gold bangles and necklaces and the men are in bowler hats and black suits. They carry cameras and sling bags, and offer gifts of almonds, scotch whisky and kosher Maggi soup cubes. 'Come to Israel,' they say, 'it is wonderful. Almonds and chicken, so cheap, so good.'

We are shown colour photographs of our cousins. The bait is dangled. Smiling faces in shorts, the family car, the kitchen, the television set, the dishwasher, the washing machine and the living room with the inevitable Mysore elephant beneath the plaque with the verse from Omar Khayyam about the loaf of bread, the glass of wine and thou...India?

And then the wedding photographs are passed around. Rarely are the brides and grooms from non-Indian families. The tradition continues—of brothers, of sisters. That is why perhaps we still continue to address each other so. Samuel says we sound like a John Wayne western. They take group photographs with Granny, kiss her and cry, remembering their parents, old houses, events, weddings. Old family quarrels are settled and at last they find release from marinating guilts. I always hear the same sigh, 'Now I will go back with a lighter heart.' They go sightseeing and secretly on the pavement of Mission Church near Ellis bridge, they look for the fortune-teller of their younger days, shyly bringing out frayed horoscopes from handbags and trying to find release from their fears of the future.

When they return after holidaying in Kashmir, they speak of future trips to Europe and America. They sometimes make us feel like poor cousins and we can never decide whether they envy or pity us.

When they leave, Granny holds our hands, looks into our eyes and cries out passionately, 'I am too old, but you are younger. Go, go to Israel.' Father looks at her angrily and says, 'Leave them alone, Ma. We'll live and die here. In India.'

Granny does not answer.

I think she is like our Hebrew prayers, often forgotten, yet, always resurfacing in our sensibilities.

Aunty Jerusha has changed. She is paranoid about being robbed and believes that people are scheming to destroy her.

She locks up everything, including the sugar, and three huge brass locks hang on the outer door when she goes out with Granny. When she leaves Granny alone in the house, she instructs her to bolt the door and not open it to anybody.

In a circle of closed doors and windows Granny plays with the phantoms of her past. The open courtyard is a distant dream and we speak of the old house in the old city like a discarded grandmother.

The last of the walls bordering the city has crumbled further and one of the shaking minarets has been closed down. Towers of illusion, which create sensations of movement. It is a mystery of the seen and unseen world. Like Samuel's questions and mine. There are never any answers.

Father, who now belongs to the council of elders says, 'Faith is the only answer.'

mandakini

In January when the sun changes direction on Uttrayan, Samuel's school friend Manu invites us to fly kites on his terrace in a pol near Raipur Darwaza.

If it weren't for Samuel, I would never have known Mandakini, Manu's sister. She studies in a

Gujarati school. She is dark, small and graceful, with large eyes lined with kajal. She wears a saffron-coloured dot between her brows instead of a red one and always seems to be barefoot, anklets jingling as she moves with an unconscious feline grace. It is a mystery why she always wears her white school dress, even on holidays. Her long plaits are tied in 'U's around her ears, with red satin ribbons that look like shoe-flowers blossoming at the edge of her dark eyebrows.

Mandakini is friendly and outspoken. She rushes down the stairs to bring us sesame laddus and Samuel says, 'She has spontaneity.' 'She is just a Maniben, a frump,' Malkha sniggers under the shadow of her straw hat, then turns to me and says, 'You better be careful, you have the makings of one.' It is winter but my face burns and Samuel pretends to be busy tying the tricky kinnas on the kites. Her comment is typical of our convent school upbringing.

Malkha finds the atmosphere alien and leaves, much to our relief. Immediately, we take off our shoes and shriek with joy every time we 'cut' the line of another kite.

We are invited often to Manu's house for celebrations but Samuel avoids inviting them to his own home. He could not possibly bear Aunty Hannah scrutinising a girl he likes.

Malkha taunts him about falling in love with an illiterate girl and they do not speak to each other. I cannot help arguing with her, 'Should we also call Granny an illiterate because she does not speak English?' As usual, she just gives me a disdainful look and reproaches me for 'talking like that about Granny'. Secretly I tell Samuel that Malkha is a snob.

Mandakini is very religious and wants to find salvation on earth itself. Following the strict Jain tradition, she eats before

turban? He would not have dared to dream of such foolishness, the family would have disowned him.

I suppose the life of a nun must be better than that of the Dariapur beggar, whom I see again as the procession passes by. I have grown older but she seems ageless, as she sits on the roadside, cupped hands stretched out from the folds of her sari. For a second she reaches out to pick up a coin Mandakini has thrown in her direction. Like Banyanbaba's pol nothing seems to change in the old city.

As the procession passes through Dilhi Darwaza and moves towards the temples on the Shahibagh road, I keep searching for Mani near her favourite bidi shop.

Only I know what is happening to Samuel. He has nightmares. He walks in his sleep and tries to jump out of the window to catch the kites he had flown with Mandakini. Aunty Hannah sits by his pillow, crying and holding him, trying to cool his burning forehead with napkins soaked in eau de cologne. Uncle Menachem watches him as though he understands everything, but does not say a word. For Aunty Hannah's benefit he says the loo, the hot summer wind, has entered the boy's brain. He concocts a mixture for him from the juice of boiled green mangos, sugar and salt, but Samuel remains delirious and refuses to heal. I am amazed that he only mumbles about kites in his sleep, and Mandakini's name never escapes his lips.

jhulta minara

 Malkha is studying
psychology in her first
year at college. She is of
the opinion that ever since little
Benjamin was born, Samuel does
not receive as much attention as he
would like, so falling ill is his way
of getting it.

And Benjibaba, growing up all
alone in the little cluttered

apartment will perhaps never know how it feels to live as part of a joint family in a big sprawling house. He vaguely relates his Jewishness to his circumcision. Later he might want to know who he is, and where he comes from and try to understand what it means to lead a lonely life, with his aging parents in a land of so many castes. He will probably never have answers, or even ask questions, because there will be a whole world of difference between him and us. I feel sorry for his smallness and loneliness. There is no reason to feel jealous of Benjibaba with his chubby cheeks and ready smile. I wish I had a brother of my own like him.

Granny tries to tell Mother that she could still have another child, but she blushes and refuses to discuss the subject. Granny tells her, 'You should not be ashamed of becoming pregnant. In our family, our women have always given birth to more than ten children. In fact my brother Gerard's wife and our mother delivered babies at the same time on the same day. It is another matter how many survive and how many miscarriages you have. But it is important for preserving our Jewishness. How else do you think we could have survived?' Granny continues, 'It's not only us. Even Subhadra's mother had another child after the girl died and treats her as a reincarnation. Look at Bilkisbibi, she is always in the maternity hospital, competing with her daughters.'

Mother touches my hair lovingly and says she has different beliefs. As it is, she finds it difficult to bring up one child, leave alone ten!

Granny gives her a suspicious glance and ends the topic with, 'You are sort of modern, always a little different from us.'

Samuel miraculously improves when I visit him with Pratibha and Vatsala. I suppose like all men he is fickle, and is now attracted to Vatsala. I wonder whether my Baghdadi Krishna is also mesmerising some blue-eyed gopi, beyond the seven seas.

For me these are difficult times.

Samuel has finished school, and insists on studying in Bombay. The council of elders is called and Aunty Jerusha supports him. Reluctantly Uncle Menachem agrees, but Aunty Hannah cries for three full days, till he agrees to write every day and keep away from girls of other communities. He is being sent to a hostel and I know we will never see him again. Even if we do, I suppose we will be like strangers.

I am lost without Samuel. Only his violin is with me. Suddenly he seems not to care for me. He is no longer protective, possessive or jealous. His weekly letter to Aunty Hannah ends with love to me, included in the 'all'. I lament his loss. We were like the shaking minarets. Our emotions were connected by the veins of blood, flowing from one to the other.

Before he left for Bombay, we had gone to Sidi Bashir's mosque beyond Kalupur Darwaza. The minarets had suddenly come alive, just for a second, and then died away.

Every time someone leaves, something breaks inside me. It was the same with the house at Dilhi Darwaza, Subhadra, my little clay Hanuman, Danieldada, Mani and now, Samuel.

the first spinster

I need Granny but it is difficult to meet her every day. Our families visit her once a month. Sometimes together, sometimes separately. Whenever I see her, I find her looking older and bent, her gait slower, the wrinkles deeper, and her skin more delicate, fine like crumpled silk. But she always reminds us to kiss the mezuzah on her doorpost before we enter the house. In our own homes, we have forgotten to kiss the sign that keeps out the night birds.

As time passes, she seems continuously bedridden. When we sit around her she asks for her spectacles in a feeble voice, then reaches with trembling hands for the old photographs hidden under her pillow and tells us stories about her brothers and sisters and their sons and daughters who have died or left for Israel and laments her inability to see them. According to her, they are leading good Jewish lives while we seem to have no sense of religion. She insists that we leave for the Promised Land and take Aunty Jerusha along. Granny worries about her all the time and Father and Uncle Menachem promise to take care of her, knowing fully well that it would be impossible to live with her. Granny hopes she will find a good man in Israel and we cannot help giggling.

Aunty flares up at Granny who quickly changes the subject to Father's business. The tension between them makes me feel sorry for Granny. Yet, that was exactly how it was destined to be. Her walking stick has thorns, or is it the other way round? Aunty Jerusha has grown more and more eccentric. Her french roll is an untidy bird's nest under which she tries to hide a bald patch.

Granny realizes that there is no longer any place for her in the houses of Menachem or Joshua. Mother says that Granny is almost ninety and may live to touch a century or more because her spirit wants to protect Aunty Jerusha from the bad world.

But why does someone as soft and loving as Granny have to drink? Every evening she drowns herself in her memories. Her

eyes sparkle and her mood changes. The laughter turns to tears.
Despite what Mother says I know she has not ruined homes but
has linked us together. The family makes sure that nobody sees
her like that, and Mother condemns Granny's weakness with a
single contemptuous word—habit.

The subject is taboo. But the question remains: why does
Granny have to drink? What is she trying to remember or forget?

Is it death or is it life ?

She is restless in the evenings, till she pours herself some
whisky, then she gets drunk and finally dozes off on the cane
chair and one of us puts her to bed.

Granny has locked herself up in Aunty Jerusha's house, and
whisky is their only solace. She sometimes sighs like Mani and
says how difficult it is to be a woman. She feels women are
imprisoned within rules, traditions and appearances. It is
impossible to crush all your desires and live. The only escape is
in forgetfulness.

Does Granny want to be herself? Is she trying to forget that
she had been a young girl of thirteen at the time of her marriage
and that she had grown up in her husband's house, yearning for
her own mother? Perhaps she had wanted to step out of the
closed courtyard to become a part of the world outside, but had
not been allowed to do so. After all, she was her husband's rib.

Her Jewishness had been nurtured in the closed courtyard
and she had been guarded against alien influences. She had
given birth to sons who were circumcised and daughters to whom
she taught the rules of being good Jewish women. Sad were the
days when the kaddish had to be read for a dead child. How

many children had she borne, and what had happened to them?
We do not know. The burden of the Jewish house had been
hers, and she had been held responsible for the faults of the
children till Grandfather died of a heart attack, leaving her to
Aunty Jerusha whom Granny seemed to have protected against
a fate akin to her own. She never said if it was fair or unfair.
Imprisoned within herself she had found an escape.

On the way back home, Mother hugs me and whispers, 'Will
you look after me in my old age ?'

'Of course, I will,' I reassure her, although the thought of
living like Aunty Jerusha frightens me.

I envy the boys who are allowed to escape. In any case, nothing
would have held them back. But if the right match is not found
for a girl she is destined to become her parents' support, for her
own good, so that she does not become polluted by sex.

I am sure some half-hearted attempts are made to get us
married, so that our parents do not feel the burden of guilt on
their souls. The most unsuitable proposals are being put forth
to Malkha, because they know very well she will refuse to consider
them. And those they think she might accept are being kept a
secret. Whenever Malkha refuses a proposal, Uncle Menachem
seems relieved that she will be free to look after them.

My life will fall into the same pattern as Aunty Jerusha's. I
feel I must speak to someone about this problem, but it is
impossible to talk to either Malkha or Aunty Jerusha. They never
disclose their inner thoughts. Perhaps I could speak to Father,
but I am almost sure he will tell me that I must do exactly as
Mother, the protector of my virginity, says. Lately there have
been discussions about the swing. Mother thinks that it is old

fashioned and should be removed and the open verandah converted into a modern living room with French windows. I am not supposed to have an opinion on the matter and cannot say that it would be a disaster to change anything in the house.

Nobody uses the swing, so my books stay there, like a private library enveloped in the fragrance of the old house and memories of Danieldada. Sometimes I read the parts I like, but on many a hot afternoon, I just doze on the swing with the smell of old books around me.

Mother wants to clear the mess and says, 'This is just your way of showing off, because in truth you never read anything except film magazines.'

I swallow the hurt. Books from Uncle Menachem's dismantled library are my only legacy from the old house at Dilhi Darwaza. When they shifted, he had to choose between them and the harmonium. There had been no space, so he had kept a few of his favourite books in a cardboard box on the mezzanine floor and donated the rest to his old school. That was the only day I had seen tears in his eyes. Then, much to Aunty Hannah's irritation, he had asked me to take the ones that I wanted. I chose the books with the best feel, texture and smell.

I am suddenly reminded of Granny's story of the Ahmedabad railway lines, of how parts of the city walls and gates had been destroyed to lay new lines and roads, to connect the old city with Bombay.

The city has opened up, but a city without walls has its own dangers. 'What is the use of gates, when there are no walls?' Granny always asks. To me her questions are like riddles.

I feel a sense of danger and insecurity. I want to hold on to the swing but am helpless. One evening when I return from school it is no longer there, and neither are my friends, the peacocks and the parrots. Like my memories of Danieldada, I bury the images deep inside me. Anyway, it was just a silly old swing. I dare not show any displeasure to Mother but I never again touch the books she has carefully arranged in the living room. I want to scream, but meet her probing glance with a smile and thank her, saying that they look beautiful in the new bookcase.

I suppose one must leave behind what is old and go ahead. This, I guess, applies only to things and not to people.

I feel like the king who tried to build the inner sanctum of the old city, against the wishes of Manekbaba, a wise old man, who made quilts. All that was built during the day fell apart at night, because he would undo the stitches on his quilt. My problem is that I cannot find my Manekbaba to resolve the curse. My world is becoming like the tale of Manekchowk, and what I try to create by day collapses at night.

the letter game

 Aunty Sinora, Mother's sister from Bombay, comes into my life when we are passing through a severe 'dress' crisis. She embarrasses Mother by criticising my clothes and insists that she be allowed to buy me 'proper' dresses, a word that seems to sting Mother. They also have secret discussions on whether or not I should be allowed to remove the fine hair on my legs and underarms. The stray words which fall on my ears make my heart jump. At last I will be allowed to have clothes like other girls of my age. Mother resists and Aunty Sinora loses the battle. She ends the conflict by saying the obvious, 'She is your daughter, do as you wish.'

'Rebel,' advises her son, James. 'It's your life.'

I cannot hurt Mother. She loves me and Father says she does everything for my own good.

At the end of her vacation Aunty Sinora gives me a pink Lucknowi salwar kameez with an odhni to match. 'This is much better than the clothes she usually wears and she needs to do something about her hair,' she says before leaving. If she had stayed longer, they would have ended up quarrelling over me.

The secrets of her life which Danieldada had kept hidden, in a plastic bag in the cupboard, reveal themselves. She is happy with the life she has made for herself, yet sad that her father never accepted her marriage. The same feeling had been evident in Aunty Julekha's tears at her father's grave.

Later I put away the pink Lucknowi dress with the anklets Danieldada gave me and Aunty Julekha's gift of another salwar kameez—a bright peacock blue with gold embroidery and a dupatta with gold sequins. 'It is too filmi,' Mother said.

Her visit had been more emotional than that of Aunty Sinora's. She had flown down from Delhi to see Mother on her way to Bombay. She was dressed in a sari and surprised Mother with her deep knowledge of Muslim traditions. Yet, once a year she prays at the synagogue on their mother's death anniversary.

Aunty Julekha had converted to the Muslim faith after marrying Iqbal Uncle when she was still in school. 'I did it because of my in-laws, and it does not matter to me whether I am called Julie or Julekha. What is important is that I am me. I am neither Jewish nor Muslim, but just a human being,' which immediately seemed to strike a chord in Father who could not help asking, 'How will you die? Because I think I will die a Jew.'

She did not answer.

Behind her face, I saw a terrible past, full of conflicts, worse than mine. Like Jacob and the angel, Julie and Julekha will always be fighting inside Aunty's body asking her, What is thy name ?

But in this one rare moment in Mother's life when she is trying to come to terms with her sisters, she is having trouble with Father's family. Her non-Jewish sisters annoy Aunty Hannah who is afraid that these outside influences might pollute her family. They stop speaking to each other; then, after a week of tension, they exchange letters through their respective cooks, who sit quietly on the floor, sipping tea from a saucer and munching khari biscuits while the answers are being written and the misunderstandings cleared up.

This is a common practice between the two women. This particular letter game had started with Aunty Hannah's objection to Mother calling Father by his first name. Like Granny, Aunty never calls her husband by name, always referring to him as 'ey' or 'Samuel's father'.

Mother had given a written explanation to Aunty Hannah, 'Joshua is my equal. I am not his slave and he is not my master that I cannot call him by his name.'

An offended Aunty Hannah had asked in return, 'Are you implying that I am my husband's slave?'

Mother's reply was, 'Perhaps not. But it is time we learnt to stand shoulder to shoulder with men and treat each other as individuals instead of differentiating between men and women.'

A cooler Aunty Hannah had retorted, 'But we were brought up to believe that if we call the father of our children by name, some evil might come upon him.'

Mother's reply was, 'These are rules made by men to keep women under control. Just call Brother Menachem by his name, nothing will happen. Look at us, we are fine.'

Aunty had been convinced but had never broken her own rules.

About her sisters, Mother writes back, 'I know you will not like such comparisons, but it is similar to the parable of the prodigal son. Does one close the door against those who wish to return home?'

Aunty Hannah asks in return, 'Do they really want to return home?'

Mother answers, 'So what should I have done ?'

At last Uncle Menachem intervenes and scribbles at the end of Aunty Hannah's long letter : Considering that we are such a small community, we have to stick together and welcome those who have left our fold so that they may still remain a part of us.

At a hastily organized dinner at Granny's, the two women cry in each other's arms.

Granny majestically proclaims, 'If the mother is a Jew it is all right, the children are automatically Jewish. The problem is more for the boys. We have to make concessions, otherwise our small community will disappear.' She looks at Uncle Menachem and says, 'But then, you do not encourage cousin marriages, do you?'

Uncle Menachem is not in a mood to discuss the issue.

Later, when they are in the kitchen, Aunty Hannah tells Mother that she is worried about Samuel. He does not write long letters. Sometimes he does not write at all, and however hard he tries, Uncle is unable to persuade Samuel to return to Ahmedabad. Mother asks suspiciously whether it is because of the girls there.

'No,' says Aunty Hannah, 'it is more to do with Samuel himself. Always too many questions and that Mandakini, horrible girl. I think she put something in the food he ate there, so his mind is disturbed. You know the time he stopped eating meat, I thought he was going to convert.'

I feel my face burn as I wait for Aunty Jerusha to open the lock of the cupboard where she keeps the plates. She tells me how she cannot trust anybody, even Granny, who gives things away to the servants if she looks the other way. She looks deep into my eyes and says, 'These are hard times.' I suppose she feels burdened with Granny, the house, her clinic and the fact that she is the breadwinner. Having buried her body under the gravestone called 'responsibility', she has been left with no emotional support.

I tell Malkha that I would hate to be another Aunty Jerusha and she whispers back to me, 'Things could be different but only if you can find a man like Uncle or Father...' I think she has a point. 'Most of the men are leaving for Israel,' she continues, 'and those who are here are not good enough for us or our family. Besides, none of them is going to spread the word in

Bombay that here we are, looking for two handsome boys in the image of Judah Ben Hur. Intelligent, educated, grooms with good manners 'Dilhi Darwaza style', for two virtuous virgins of Ahmedabad city in the state of Gujarat who speak three languages and no Marathi ! Also, remember we are like Manibens when compared with the Bombay crowd. So that's that. I advise you to forget all this, just study and make something of yourself. Look at Aunty Jerusha, at least she does not need a man. Only our work will be of any use to us.' When Malkha talks like that she sounds like the council of elders.

Uncle Gerard's family has asked for her hand again. Joel is doing well in Israel, and the council has no objections, but Malkha is hesitant.

'Joel is a dumbbell,' she says and this makes Aunty Hannah suspect that Malkha is attracted to someone else in her college.

I try to study but find it impossible to concentrate. It is my last year in school and everybody is worried for they feel I might not fare well in the examinations. Mother is ashamed of me and I keep hearing the oft-repeated reproach, 'You will come to nothing.'

mon repos

Processions spark riots. Silver paper and gold-foil buntings unfurl in a belligerent display of strength. Weapons and self-flagellation have . undertones of violence.

A small stone is thrown from the roof of a pol and anger spreads like a forest fire. Tempers rise easily and the firefly has no place in the darkness of the night when eyes keep watch and men stalk the streets armed with scythes, lathis and naked swords, avenging one another. Father says, 'These are difficult times. You brush against someone in Manekchowk and suddenly, you are bleeding at the waist.'

Drop by drop the blood collects in a pool of poison. Will it dry up or kill the tree of life that had once spread its branches over the pols? Interconnecting veins of brotherhood are being cut by knives which have the labels of gods. I haven't even found my own god and have begun to believe that they're all the same, a common karma or kismat, a common destiny, a common creator with a different name. This confuses Father's belief in humanity and in turn confuses me further. Can there be a God when all this is allowed to happen?

Father brings out the hidden air gun—till now he had used it to shoo away the langurs that sometimes vandalised the garden—and spends the nights patrolling the streets with the other men in the locality.

These are dark days. The black ants are everywhere, and unfortunately, they are not the harmless little ones which bring prosperity. These are bigger and blacker with long hooked beaks that remain embedded in the skin when they bite you. For months they have made their home under our house without our suspecting it, although at times, we had seen them walking in a line towards a dead insect. With the first monsoon, they overflow from under the pot of the touch-me-nots and spread all over the house like a soft, rippling, black carpet. Mistry pours kerosene over them, saying they will bring misfortune to the house, and Mother is hysterical when an ant crawls up her thigh.

Later that year, Father has a nervous breakdown after he loses Sulemanbhai and Hasmukh Mistry, two of his most trusted men, in the riots. One was chased down the road and stabbed, and the other was burnt alive. After attending their funerals, Father walks around the house looking lost and helpless.

'Help comes in different ways,' says Aunty Jerusha and adds, 'the Lord giveth, the Lord taketh away.'

Mohun has written a postcard to us saying that he is fine with the 'blessings of Danbaba', and Mani, who now knows how to make a telephone call from the public booth, calls to say that she is well.

One day Father wakes up from his pain and decides to train Mistry's young son Surya to take his father's place. He buys a pair of cocker spaniels and once again takes to playing the dilruba he had put away after his marriage. The dogs make him feel safer and the music heals him.

I am sad to leave the old city behind. We decide to move closer to Granny and shift to a new house in Navrangpura, across the river. We have converted two tenements into one, with an outhouse in the backyard for Mistry's family. The house has a slanting roof covered with tiles. The front verandah is crammed with wood carvings and furniture, while ornamental grills decorate the doors and windows that open onto a lawn edged with henna bushes. Mani used to apply a layer of henna paste on her feet to soothe her cracked heels.

I know it will not be easy to make friends here. We live behind high walls, with a sign on the door that says : 'Beware of Dogs'.

The house feels like a cage but Father says, 'In these difficult times we should do all that we can to ensure our safety.'

Danieldada's cottage was smaller than the house in Dilhi Darwaza, but it definitely had much more open space than our new house, which Father has named Mon Repos.

The house in Shahibagh had four rooms which were interconnected, and when I was younger Mother would sometimes chase me through them, ruler in hand, and I would avoid being caught by running in circles, through all the four rooms. The doors opened onto the verandah with the swing, where the strong fragrance of raat ki rani, queen of the night, filled the air. A woven bamboo screen served as our garden wall. In summer, we slept under mosquito nets near the pond where I had buried my little Hanuman. That was before the Kesuda tree stopped blossoming and Mother sold the swing.

The house in Navrangpura is different. It has an iron gate with a doorbell fixed to the wall, but most people prefer to rattle the iron latch like they used to at our Dilhi Darwaza house. Cutting across the lawn, a mosaic pathway leads to an enclosed verandah, beyond which is the drawing room where Father's favourite Omar Khayyam plates, paintings and sculptures are on display.

A staircase leads to a room upstairs, stacked with unsold furniture and things from the old house. We sleep on the terrace during the hot summer months. Strangely enough, nothing seems to survive here except the acacia tree under which Father has built a kennel for Lassie and Leo.

The silence of the house breaks when the langurs, squirrels and peacocks visit us.

Mani has returned to us. Her husband died of a heart attack when their house was burnt down and she did not know where else to go. She is homeless like the Dariapur beggar who seems to have disappeared. She is not the same, but it is good to have her back. There are so many stories in her silence. But she looks exactly as she did before she remarried. The colour of her sari is still a mystery and she sits hunched within its folds after her work is done.

I lose her again when Mother decides to set her up with Aunty Jerusha who has driven away her twelfth maid, accusing her of theft. Mother feels it is better that Mani stays with her in the locked house because Aunty is familiar with her. I am helpless. I realise that somehow the old Mani does not fit into Mother's new set-up. Mani leaves with a silent salaam, without even the flicker of an eyelid.

river of tears

other is sure I will not pass my school examinations and till my results appear in the local newspaper, we are all tense. I pass, but unlike Aunty Jerusha who would certainly have topped the class, I am at the bottom of the list.

The family's honour is salvaged.

In college, Sanskrit interests me. I like to read the epics and Kalidasa. But I keep away from Kama and his arrows, lest he come between my parents and me. My teachers are surprised at my interest in the ancient language. They like listening to the perfect recitation of slokas by somebody with an unmistakably Biblical name like mine. I gain confidence, and although pleased with my progress, Mother cannot come to terms with my decision not to eat meat. I refuse to help her pluck the chicken and she never knows what to cook for me. I cook my own vegetables and shock her further by wearing white sarees with the pallav arranged on the right shoulder in the Gujarati style. She is convinced I have been hypnotized by my professors and forces me to change colleges. I resist and she asks me if I have decided to convert. Finally, I give in and take up psychology instead of Sanskrit and this resolves the tension in the house.

I feel distressed. Only Granny heals me when I touch the crumpled silk of her skin, and when I look into her eyes, I remember the Shabbat prayers at the Dilhi Darwaza house. This image has always sparked in me a desire for the Jewish life that Granny had managed to keep alive with a candle, a star and the Shema Israel; the fragrance of freshly baked bread, homemade grape wine, rice flour sandans in the tandoor and chicken boiling in green coriander curry. It is now something distant, an inaccessible something that is out my reach and I ache for it.

Granny has become insistent that we go to Israel and there is an urgency in her voice.

One day, quietly, she dies in her sleep.

Stone-faced, Aunty Jerusha sits next to her body and starts talking to herself in incoherent, disjointed phrases.

We are inconsolable.

Uncle Menachem and Father are as lifeless as pillars as they go through the rituals for the funeral. Mani holds Aunty Jerusha back as she tries to stop her brothers from taking Granny to the graveyard. Mani then consoles me and says if I cry so much, Granny will find it difficult to come back to us for she will not be able to cross the river of tears. She is sure Granny will return after forty days if I fulfil at least one of her unrealised wishes. Perhaps I should go to Israel.

The family feels orphaned.

Uncle Menachem sits at the table in a state of shock because Samuel has refused to come home for the funeral. In Benjibaba, standing still with the candle, I see Samuel's face.

The walls have fallen and like the gates of the city we stand exposed, vulnerable and defenceless.

star of david

 Mother buries Father every day, and denies life in her fear of his death.

Kali scares me with the sound of drums and brass bells and I try to escape through the tunnel under the Bhadra fort. But this time there is no escape. One morning, Father disappears, and Mother cries all day long for she is sure that he has deserted her for another woman. When he does not return that night, I feel homeless but in the face of Mother's agony, I do not show my despair. In a strange way he symbolises everything that is home far more than Mother does.

A message is sent to Uncle Menachem and he too joins us in our vigil for Father. I notice that he never once offers Mother any sympathy and is impatient with her for crying. Yet, he feels burdened with responsibility because he does not want to inform the police. It would bring shame to the family. At midnight he forces Mother to take a tranquilizer and go to bed. He himself lies down in the drawing room but I know that he stays awake all night.

In the morning Father joins us for breakfast as though nothing has happened. One has to laugh with him. His hair is tousled, and he smells of the forest and looks so cheerful that it is impossible to cry or be angry with him. He does not pay attention to Mother's frozen stare. He had spent the night alone at the mouth of the Sabarmati, watching fireflies, and listening to the sounds of birds and insects. After that incident, Mother is always wary of Father and a curtain of silence hangs between them. Mother is offended because he had not confided in her.

Perhaps she does not believe him and suspects that he has cheated her, just as Danieldada had cheated Grandmother Leah. She feels defeated by Father and me. For the first time I feel sorry for her and want to hold her the way I had once wanted her to hold me.

The library is my only escape. Mother and Father have differences of opinion over various things and the house is never quiet. Father is no longer dependent on Mother and tends to be aggressive, and Mother suspects that Father is meeting another woman although she is not sure who she is. Father tries to flatter Mother by calling her a goddess. By placing her on a pedestal he has given himself the freedom of mortals. This makes her even more suspicious. His silence makes her irritable. Behind the brown tones, the colours are veiled. One does not know what the other is thinking.

To be shut up with them in the house during the holidays is like drowning in a well. I have to run away somewhere and I need Mani who is now living with Aunty Jerusha.

Mani sits huddled outside Aunty's door. Her eyes are expressionless as she looks up at me and they do not warm with pleasure as they used to. Often Aunty throws her out of the house on the suspicion that she has stolen sugar or ghee and Mani, homeless and bereft, sits for hours outside the door, until Aunty needs her again. She goes through this ritual without complaint.

After I ring the doorbell and call out to her, I hear Aunty Jerusha walking to the door and fumbling with the two big brass locks, muttering something about being disturbed when she is busy. The door is opened and then closed on my face.

As I turn to leave, the door opens again and Aunty Jerusha stands in the doorway, wrapped in a blue silk kimono with a red dragon running across it. Her face is plastered with powder like a geisha's and one of her moth-eaten French scarves adorns her balding scalp. Though it is the height of summer, she is wearing her ancient fur-tufted bedroom slippers with the Made in

England tags still hanging from the corners. She leans over and kisses me, reeking of rum, moth balls and perspiration and I realise that she has probably not had a bath in days. As soon as I enter her house, she shuts the door and complains about Mani who waits outside.

I sit at the dining table in the kitchen and watch Aunty Jerusha unlock her meat safe, take out Granny's gold jewellery and spread it on the table. I stare wide-eyed at the pearl earrings, the gold bangles and wedding ring, the delicate gold necklace and the Star of David, the silver armlets, toe rings and the anklets which make me think of Danieldada.

She gives me the Star of David as if she were offering me some of her favourite Ravalgaon toffees and tells me to hide it in my bag. She does not want Mani to know about it. Little does she know that Mani's most precious possession, her perfume box, lies unopened under my saris, waiting for my wedding day.

She quickly unlocks the door again and tells Mani to buy three cups of kesar ice cream, which we eat together, Mani included. There is a slight hint of amusement in Mani's eyes as she looks at me.

I am in a strange dilemma. Mother dislikes gold, silk and chiffon; for her they symbolise sin and are reminders of her mother's valley of death. She has never allowed me to touch any of them, and says that it is unfair to wear jewellery because of the poverty around us. One can do nothing in the house without taking Mother's permission and nothing can be hidden from her prying eyes.

The Star must disappear into the tiny red box under the saris, like my anklets and Mani's perfume box. Mother is of the opinion that one need not wear one's Jewishness for all the world to see, it is something that glows in the heart. It is difficult to understand or oppose Mother's ideas. Yet it is good to feel the Star when I am confused. It has Granny's touch and I feel warm in its presence. I keep telling myself that some day I shall wear it, maybe after Mother's death.

I wonder why the Star was chosen as an auspicious symbol. Perhaps at dusk the North Star had brought solace to the Jews wandering by day under the hot desert sun and it was their symbol of hope. Or was it the falling star, restless, fluid and sensuous, melting into the darkness of the earth. Or did it come from India, through Mesopotamia or the Indus, the female element and the male element, dissolving into each other, moving through centuries and turning into a yellow piece of cloth, stitched on the heart and dipped in blood. I wonder why Granny always referred to the Star as her Zion.

I feel safe with my Star, but the triangles of the male and female bother me, casting long shadows on my life.

under curfew

We're all much older now. Aunty Jerusha lives in a haunted house. She has closed down her clinic and sits inside the house with all the doors locked. Losing keys and finding them is her favourite pastime. She holds long dialogues with Granny as though they are still sleeping together in the same room. The white ants grow like tall creepers in her house, the way they have grown into her brain.

For her, Jerusalem is still a distant dream and Ahmedabad is an illusion. She wants to be buried next to Granny, just as Father wants to be buried next to Mother and Aunty Hannah next to Uncle Menachem. Perhaps Malkha and I, the virgin spinsters, could be buried next to each other.

But it is Samuel who decided to lay himself to rest under the sun on a tarred road, hungry and full of some drug known only to him. Granny would have said, 'It is all because of too much education and the freedom to mingle with other communities. Had that been controlled, you would not have lost him. The parents are responsible, not allowing cousins to marry. All these modern views are no good for us.'

The day his body was brought back and wrapped in the traditional shroud we had stitched ourselves, Ahmedabad was under curfew. We raced through the kaddish as Benjibaba stood over the grave just as Samuel had once stood over Danieldada's grave, with the wax that dripped from the candle burning his hands, tears running down his cheeks for a brother he had hardly known. He is different, our Benjibaba. Tall and quiet, and ever watchful, he never asks questions, and is not encouraged to do so. He works hard at school and Aunty Hannah says proudly that he is brilliant.

I am sure he suffers like us. Aunty Hannah says that she does not know him any more. He does not argue about anything nor does he create scenes and unlike us, he informs the family about his decisions only after he makes them. And Aunty, scared that Benjamin might follow in Samuel's footsteps, allows him all the freedom he wants and protects him from Uncle's periodical furies.

Ever since Samuel's death, Uncle does not work as he used to before. The family finances are running low, and Benjibaba takes the opportunity to ask for his father's consent to leave on a youth aliyah group to Israel. He tells his aging parents quietly that he sees no future for himself either with them or in India. The slide-shows and talks on Israel he attends have influenced him. Uncle agrees to let him go. For once the council of elders is not called and everybody assumes the role of saviour in trying to help Benjamin escape to the Promised Land.

I am surprised to see him so distant, dry-eyed and without emotion and it looks as though we will never hear from him again. Another son crosses over the sea of Aunty Hannah's tears. Uncle Menachem signs the necessary papers and blesses him without emotion as Malkha holds her mother in her arms and says, 'I will never leave you.'

wailing walls

A sultan once saw a rabbit turn on an attacking dog, where the Kankaria lake now stands and this convinced him that it would be the ideal site to build a city—a place such as this, where even something as timid as a rabbit could fight a dog. That was the day that Ahmedabad was conceived in a vision of violence. The roles are being reversed all the time: strange animals, half-rabbit, half-dog, each eating the other.

Curfew, riots, bloodshed. A river of tears separates us from one another. All that remains of the walls of the old city is a crumbling mound of bricks. I think of it as Ahmedabad's Wailing Wall; it watches over the tears of its people. Nobody visits it or prays to it for help and not even the pigeons find sanctuary in its crevices. Perhaps rats and ants have made their homes at its base. Perhaps Ahmedabad's soul still lives here. Perhaps it is dying like an old grandmother and it needs our help or perhaps it could help us.

The gates stand like lone sentinels with nothing to protect. The curfew slithers between one gate and the other like a constricting python entangled in heavy military boots, guns, water cannons and tear gas. There is no traffic on the roads and in the silence, there is a threat. Who is the victim and who the aggressor, one cannot tell.

The Sabarmati becomes the focus of a strange exodus. There are families searching for a corner where they can be safe. The river separates us from the old city, in the same way that it had separated us from Granny. It looks like a river of blood with cloth dyers washing red cloth in a dying river. Crossing it becomes important. There are questions and more questions churning inside our minds. What is good? What is safe? We live in conflict.

shakti

hen I think of Dilhi Darwaza, I invariably think about Emmanuel. He writes long letters to Uncle Menachem, who reads them aloud to us. They are interesting accounts of his conflict, about being a Jew in a strange land. He also writes about the problems he has been having with his simple wife Queenie, who, shocked at his devotion to other gods had sent their two children to her parents' house, as she had not wanted their father's eccentricities to influence them. Later, she too left him after he'd tried a tantric experiment on her, and reached her mother's house in a hysterical state. Mother says that we were lucky not to have accepted Emmanuel's proposal. 'Think how horrible your fate would have been,' she adds. I am not sure what to think.

Emmanuel has quit his job as a professor in order to be closer to his guru in Ahmedabad, and the family is in a state of shock. It is assumed that he will stay with Uncle Menachem till he finds a house and Aunty Hannah has made a master plan to guard Malkha's virginity because she does not trust Emmanuel. According to her, a married man without a woman is a dangerous animal.

But Aunty Hannah need not have worried about Malkha. Emmanuel is still interested in me. Mother aborts all his plans to see me alone and whenever he is invited home, she makes sure never to leave the room even for a second. He speaks to me about religion and Father and Mother sit beside us in silence. I feel as if Samuel has returned, but have to hide my feelings from Mother or she would never allow me to meet him.

On the pretext of finding work at the university, Emmanuel comes to see me there, and I, knowing that Father and Mother are not at home, invite him for lunch. As Mother always keeps saying, perhaps I still have the devil in me.

We eat cold chapatis with stuffed brinjals, and I enjoy talking to him, till he takes my oily fingers in his and asks me to marry him. The beginnings of a dusty damri make the dry leaves dance outside and I am reminded of the day Samuel proposed to me. When I rise to close the windows, he misunderstands my intentions. 'So, it means yes?' he asks, holding my hands again. 'You have been the image of Shakti for me and I have always dreamt of you as my partner.' I feel my body open and close again, and I am suddenly wide awake with the fear of the future and of the condemnation of the family. I have to refuse his offer and all temptation must be squashed. I quickly push his hand away and order him to leave, my eyes stern behind the thick frame of my glasses, my hair intact in the coil of the chignon, my sari wrapped around me like a bandage. And then, I add in a trembling voice, 'You are like my brother Samuel, how can you...'

emmanbaba and queeniemummy

Emmanuel works as an insurance agent from his house in a suburban housing society and we rarely see him anymore. He wears rings of semi-precious stones to ward off the influence of certain planets and tells us that he has converted one of the rooms in his house into a pooja room. He has turned vegetarian, fasts sometimes, practises yoga, and goes around in a purple bathrobe, with a shawl thrown over his shoulders. Uncle Menachem refers to him as Emmanbaba.

There is no sign of Queenie, and like a gandharva from swarg he marries Kamla, the young widow he has met at the local satsang, by exchanging garlands in front of the gods in his pooja room. The elders shake their heads helplessly and Uncle Menachem laments, 'One more of us has gone astray.'

I am relieved but worry about whether I could have saved him. As soon as Kamla gives birth to a son, we receive a basket of bundi laddus covered with silver foil and a note from Emmanuel saying that he has circumcised his son in a private hospital. Uncle Menachem is relieved and says, 'Good he did not miss the eighth day.' The family sends a silver rattle for the child, wishing him peace and prosperity. But rumour has it that one of the elders from the community had circumcised the boy in the synagogue, and Emmanuel's first wife Queenie had been present to play mother.

A strange story unfolds. It is true that a reluctant Queenie has been pressurised to return to her husband's house. She calls on Mother one Sunday afternoon, when we are dozing on the living room carpet after a good lunch of puris and mango juice.

I have never seen Queenie before and when she whispers her name, I thank God for having had the sense to refuse Emmanuel's offer; I could never have forgiven myself had I hurt this simple and helpless woman.

Small and timid in a rose-pink polyester sari, she sits huddled on the sofa, wiping her eyes with a purple handkerchief. Her hair is thin and plaited into a small rope-like braid which makes her look bald. Her body is soft, round and shapeless and her face is all cheeks with a huge nose sticking out. Her small eyes shine like the Star of David around her neck.

I pretend to sleep, and hear her telling Mother how she has always been a good wife but is fated to suffer because of the bad deeds of her past births. Quietly Mother reminds her that she speaks like that because she has been influenced by Emmanbaba. There is nothing like rebirth for the Jews. 'Believe,' says Mother, 'believe in your religion, say the Shema, kiss the mezuzah and keep the evil out of your house.' I am surprised to hear Mother talk like Granny. 'How can I do that?' asks Queenie. 'Evil now lives in my house.'

Emmanuel has blackmailed Queenie's parents, threatening that if she does not return to him and play the legal parent to his son by Kamla, he would take away the children on the grounds that Queenie is hysterical and incapable of looking after them. That is the reason why Queenie had returned and helped with the circumcision of Emmanbaba's son. The community knows about this, but as Uncle Menachem says, 'It is all right as long as the tribe increases.'

When Queenie holds on to Mother and cries, 'Aunty, I wish to die,' Mother looks as if she has been struck by lightning and I sit up, bolt upright. Like the reflection from a stained glass window, snatches of Danieldada's story scatter around us. Mother looks disturbed and I fetch a glass of cold water for her. It is as if her mother's story is repeating itself and I am afraid that her blood pressure will shoot up. Queenie, naive as she is, has chosen the wrong confidante. But, perhaps not. Mother goes on to console her and tells her that at least for the sake of her children she should not do anything like that. Nobody else could take care of them like she does. 'A suicide,' says Mother, 'leaves scars for generations. Besides, in the eyes of our god, it is a sin to take one's own life. Try to find solace in your children and help them to become good human beings. At least your husband is giving you the status of the elder wife.'

After Queenie leaves, I can see that Mother is deeply troubled. Perhaps she is wondering whether Leah and Durga could have lived together. And if they had, would the daughters have adjusted to the new situation? At least it would have saved a life. After that particular incident Mother is very sympathetic towards Queenie, who in return sends Mother tiffin carriers of food and snacks. Mother also helps her find work as a typist and the two women meet regularly. For Mother, Queenie is the daughter she had hoped to find in me and for Queenie she becomes the mother.

Mother helps Queenie to recover from one crisis after another. Legally, Emmanbaba is in trouble since he has two wives. To solve the problem, he is considering becoming a Muslim. This is the last straw for Queenie. She packs her bags and gets ready to leave for Bombay. She does not even want her children any more but once again, Mother convinces her to stay. I feel like telling Mother that Queenie should not take any more nonsense from Emmanbaba, but I know how Mother will react to that. She will insist that Queenie make sacrifices for the sake of her children. The ease with which Emmanuel changes his garb from Sadhu to Pir is a matter of great surprise to the family who now cuts off all connections with him. But he does not care.

Yet, I am convinced that Emmanbaba is a lost soul, trying to search for his Jewish identity through all the religions that surround him. Queenie says that a poster with Urdu calligraphy now adorns a shelf in the drawing room. She is now close to Kamla and is proud that they are like two sisters in their common resistance against one man. Kamla is no longer evil. Emmanuel is.

They do not question his once-a-week absence. For a day the women are freed from Emman Pir's conflicts and he spends the day at the Chalte Pir ki Dargah, or sits spinning khadi at the Gandhi ashram. For once Uncle Menachem has nothing to say and I am jealous that Emmanbaba has the freedom to experiment with his life.

Whenever he disappears the women emerge stronger and take all the major decisions, but when he returns, the household recedes into melancholic silence.

Every Sunday he wears a white khadi kurta-pyjama and leaves on his bicycle without disclosing his destination.

For some reason he has discarded his eccentric robe and wears khadi. However, on Fridays he invariably asks his wife, 'Queeniebai, why haven't you lit the Shabbat candles?' Kamla usually prepares the Shabbat table and then Queenie sits at the head of the table and conducts the services, helping her son with the kiddush cup. She is no longer soft or timid and has now become Shakti, the universal mother.

Emmanuel's activities have long been a favourite topic of discussion in the family because he always does the unexpected. And now, at forty, when he is well past the age for it, Emmanbaba surprises us by celebrating his own bar mitzvah. On the way to his house, Uncle Menachem mutters, 'Now what sort of drama is this?' We enter Emmanbaba's house for the first time and as we kiss the mezuzah on the door, he beams at us, and asks us to remove our footwear. Kamla covers her head and bends down to touch the feet of the elders. I can feel Aunty Hannah transforming into a dragon.

Emmanbaba obviously has a fan following, because brothers Jhirad, Elijah and Raymond are flashing rings of semi-precious stones and discussing their horoscopes with him. Then, as an elder reads out some passages from a Marathi book, Emmanuel is given the Talith, the prayer shawl.

Lovingly he drapes it around his shoulders, weeping and saying how he has always wanted to be a good Jew, and now that he has the Talith, he promises to respect his religion. As his eyes shine, Gandhi smiles at him from a framed photograph and Queenie cannot stop laughing in the little kitchen where she is sitting on the floor, sari hitched up and feet soaking in the blood and feathers of a dozen chickens she has just made kosher.

maya

ometimes I think our story is like that of Daniel in the lion's den. The animal called desire roams around our minds and we have to win it over with love or some good deed we might have done in the past, like having given alms to the Dariapur beggar. Where she is now I do not know.

Everything is maya, and it has spun a web around us. What appears around us is not that which exists. Behind the curtain of the synagogue, in the Hebrew inscriptions on the grave, in the light of the candle, is that which we try to grasp but cannot, because that which we are looking for does not have the eyes of Shakti, mesmerizing us with belief.

Everything is maya, the illusion of so many births, so many shipwrecks, so many voyages, so many massacres. Yet one can take a dip in the Dead Sea and emerge in the Ganga having lived through a whole landscape of experiences. Perhaps Emmanbaba has understood this, perhaps not, we do not know. As Uncle Menachem says, he could be a fake.

There have been unseasonal rains and we spend many a night holding bowls of water under the pale glow of the lights, collecting thousands of dead insects which attract the lizards that cover the walls with their fat, slippery bodies.

The riots have erupted again and the poison creepers grow like huge fishing nets in the river and in lakes, devouring the last of the dying fish.

Around us is a sense of doom and whenever the curfew is lifted, Mother rushes to console Aunty Hannah. A lizard has fallen on her head and she is certain that Benjibaba is dead, just like Samuel. Malkha cannot help them. She is on the telephone trying to locate her brother.

And then Emmanbaba dies and Aunty Hannah is vaguely relieved, but she is still in a state of shock, and says death sometimes comes in threes, and wonders who will be next.

Emmanbaba had left home on his bicycle one day after the disturbances had begun and the hospitals were full of dead bodies. Queenie and Kamla had tried to stop him, but he had quietly resisted their efforts and left on what appeared to be a secret mission.

According to Kamla, he was dressed in a flapping purple bathrobe, his hair flying around his face. 'He looked like the prophet Abraham,' she sighs. He had cycled to his own death, which he himself had predicted would happen in the middle of the road. And so it had come to pass, and there he had lain in the middle of the road, near his wrecked bicycle, quietly looking at the blue sky, stabbed in the stomach.

They close his eyes with the earth from Jerusalem and lower him into the grave, his new prayer shawl draped around his shoulders. Blood flows in the dry river bed.

vishchakra

The synagogue has been silent for too long. The walls facing Jerusalem are being painted, and the windows are being repaired. The brass menorahs and glass oil lamps are being cleaned, as also the marble façade of the teva and the gold-embroidered red velvet curtains that protect the Books.

I am still searching for the focal bindu in the mysterious curtain which hides the eyes of my god. Just as our eyes search for Benjamin, our lost brother. Although his letters are full of promises, he never returns. We do not recognize the man in the colour photographs he sends us.

Malkha and I are the last of what is referred to as 'the family'. We have decided to lock our wombs, the way Aunty Jerusha has locked herself in her flat with Mani. Perhaps Malkha and I will only have each other and our memories of the old house. We will hang upside down like bats and will never know how to fly like birds. Yet, late at night, after we have tucked our parents into bed, we open the romantic novels we pick up from Teen Darwaza, and enter the cool step-wells of unknown romances. Promises of love in our next birth are our private oases, as we look at the light shining on the water deep below, out of reach.

We make an odd pair, Malkha and I, when we take an auto-rickshaw to go to the cinema together, she in her Queen Elizabeth hairstyle and long skirts, and me in my white Gujarati sari and tight chignon pulled back sternly. Arthritis and backaches torture us, but we dare not grow old because of our aging parents who sit quietly in front of the television, looking into space and thinking about the past. Mother is on a pension now. Uncle Menachem has sold his clinic and Aunty Hannah spends her days tottering in and out of the kitchen. Our aim is to keep them alive for when they die, our lives will become pointless. Look at Aunty Jerusha.

Malkha runs a secular English school in the suburbs, and
I teach at a local college. We lead separate lives, organising our
respective cooks and maids for our parents' comfort. We meet
twice a month in each other's homes, and sing old Hindi songs
with our mothers. With shaky fingers, Uncle Menachem plays his
harmonium and Father accompanies him on the dilruba. Samuel's
violin sleeps in its black sarcophagus of a case, abandoned in the
extra room upstairs.

When the old city is not under curfew, we take our parents
to the synagogue for a Shabbat, a circumcision, or a wedding.
Supporting them with our arms around their shoulders, we
stop to kiss the mezuzah as we enter the house of God. We
never leave Ahmedabad. We never can.

I have discovered that Ahmedabad has a new god. He was
born from the blood of the two virgins whose bodies had lain
naked on the freshly tarred road, waiting for the municipal
hearse to pick them up. This god has two fierce heads,
looking in opposite directions and each of his thousand hands
holds a naked sword. Now, my search for gods is over.

I am not very sure what Malkha thinks because she does
not express her feelings.

As for me, I do not wish to take a husband, because I am
afraid to beget a daughter. According to our laws she would be
Jewish and it would be torture for her and for me. I would try to
keep her away from every possible outside influence and she
would have to fight me. She would have unruly hair which I
would have to pull back in a tight braid, in order to make

her look unattractive. I would try to manipulate and control her every thought and action and her grandmother's urgent voice would beg her to go to the Promised Land. Then my unborn daughter would somehow learn to worry about me and my old age and would perhaps end up living with me, as I live with Father and Mother.

It is a vishchakra, a never-ending, poisonous cycle because she, as a daughter, would want to know all that I know, forcing me to start this story all over again.

glossary

Aarti: Adoration of the gods with lamps, bells, flowers, and other offerings.

Agarbati: Fragrant joss sticks used for rituals by almost all Indian communities.

Alta: Bright red liquid paint applied to the hands and feet of women and young girls during festivals or even in daily life as a body makeup. It is popularly used by Indian classical dancers.

Apsara: Celestial dancer portrayed in Indian temple sculpture.

Attar: Perfume made from flowers.

Bajra rotla: Handmade roasted millet bread, rolled flat like a pancake.

Bhaiya: Literally, brother, but in Gujarat this word is associated with vegetable vendors from north India.

Bhindi: Okra.

Bhoot: Ghosts.

Bidi: Tobacco rolled in a leaf; local Indian cigarette.

Bindu: Central point.

Chana ata: Chickpea flour used in Indian cuisine.

Chapati: Handmade flat, roasted, unleavened wheat bread.

Chevado: Fried puffed rice, seasoned with spices and nuts.

Chudail: Malignant female spirit.

Dada: Grandfather.

Dal: Yellow lentils cooked with spices like a soup and eaten with rice.

Damri: Dust storm.

Dilruba: Stringed musical instrument played with a bow.

Door raho: "Stay away."

Dushera: Symbolic burning of the effigy of the ten-headed demon Ravana, according to the epic Ramayana; an auspicious day for new beginnings.

Ganja: Hemp.

Ghaghra: Flared skirt of cotton, silk, or brocade generally worn by tribals or villagers but also fashionable and worn by young urban girls during festivals or weddings. The skirts can be plain, colorful, embroidered, or printed.

Ghee: Clarified butter.

Ghoda gadi: Horse carriage.

Gopis: The cowherd girls who were in love with the god Krishna, according to the epics.

Gulab jamuns: Balls of milk pastry soaked in a sugary syrup.

Hanuman: Divine monkey god from the epic Ramayana.

Hookah: Water pipe.

Jhulta minara: Shaking minarets or towers of a mosque in Ahmedabad.

Kajal: Kohl.

Kumkum: Bright vermillion dot worn by Hindu women on their foreheads. It once indicated the marital status of women, but it has become more of a fashion accessory and is worn by women of all communities.

Laddus: Round traditional sweet made with chickpea flour, semolina, or wheat flour.

Lota: All-purpose metal tumbler.

Lungi: Sarong.

Mandap: Pavilion or gateway at the entrance of a temple or house.

Masjid: Mosque.

Methi khakras: Paper-thin, brittle wheat bread—like a dry chapatti—made plain or mixed with fenugreek leaves or other herbs.

Mudra: Meaningful and codified hand gestures based on aesthetics, seen in Indian temple structures. Mudras are an important aspect of Indian classical dance.

Neem: Large tree that has medicinal properties.

Odhni: Half sari, worn around a ghaghra or flared skirt.

Paan: Betel leaf, eaten with a filling of mint and areca nut.

Pedas: Flat balls of dry milk pastry; commonly used for festivities.

Pikchur: Hindi cinema or moving pictures.

Pir: Muslim holy man.

Pooja: Prayer; adoration of the gods.

Pujari: Priest of a temple.

Rabari: The shepherd community of Gujarat.

Rakhi: Decorative cotton, satin, or silk thread tied by a sister onto her brother's wrist during a festival to assure protection from her brother.

Rakshasa: Demons, as described in the epics.

Rangoli: Powder or liquid color designs made at the entrance of the house.

Sadhu: Ascetic associated with one of the several religious sects or temples of India.

Sadhvi: Female ascetic.

Salaam: Greeting of Urdu origin.

Samosa: Triangular fritter with a spicy vegetable or meat filling.

Sati: Shiva's wife, who because of a family fued resorted to self-immolation. The term is used for a woman who immolates herself on the funeral pyre of her husband. In ancient times, Sati was practiced by women to escape invaders. For a widow the act of Sati was considered holy, and after her death, the woman was given the status of Sati or folk goddess. The Sati system has been abolished in India.

Shakti: Feminine creative energy associated with the goddess Kali.

Shivlinga: Phallic symbol associated with the god Shiva.

Sindoor: Red powder made with earth colors used to make dots for religious and marriage rituals.

Swarg: Abode of the gods of the Hindu pantheon.

Tantric: A person practicing tantra according to Hindu, Buddhist, or Jain sacred texts that deal with ancient magical practices.

Thali: Circular plate made of brass, bronze, or steel used for eating food in the traditional Indian way. Food such as rice, dry vegetables, or pickles is served directly in the plate, while liquids are served in small bowls of the same metal.

Tilak: White, red, or yellow dot applied on the forehead of both men and women during Hindu cermonies.

Vaghri: Tribal community of Gujarat.

Vibhuti: Ash smeared on the forehead and body by ascetics of certain sects.

Vishchakra: Vicious circle.